Dear Reader . . .

There's a place where life moves a little slower, where a neighborly smile and a friendly hello can still be heard. Where news of a wedding or a baby on the way is a reason to celebrate—and gossip travels faster than a telegraph! Where hope lives in the heart, and love's promises last a lifetime.

The year is 1874, and the place is Harmony, Kansas . . .

# A TOWN
# CALLED HARMONY
## AMAZING GRACE

### *Deborah James*

Dee Dee Gallagher came from Pennsylvania to see her beloved Uncle Zeke—and she's ready for a summer of fun and adventure. But is Harmony ready for *her?*

Joshua Wylie is Harmony's busy new minister, and the last thing on his mind is finding himself a wife. But Maisie Hastings and Minnie Parker have other plans for the handsome young preacher . . .

Embarking on a furious matchmaking competition, each of the sisters sends for the unmarried relation of her choice. When the proper young ladies arrive in Harmony, they make quite an impression with their pleasant manners and churchgoing ways—and everyone agrees that either candidate would make an ideal minister's wife. But Joshua can't help but notice the barber's niece, DeeDee Gallagher—after all, it would be hard to miss this lively gal who accidentally pushes Joshua into a horse trough upon their first meeting! In fact, DeeDee is forever trying to help people—and usually causes a little bedlam instead . . . Maybe it's the spirit of the Wild West from the dime novels she loves that makes her so unique. Or the buckskin and fringe she wears. Either way, it's not hard to see that DeeDee has a heart of gold. And, to the surprise of most everyone in town, Reverend Wylie thinks she might just be his perfect match . . .

# Welcome to
# A TOWN
# CALLED HARMONY . . .

**MAISIE HASTINGS & MINNIE PARKER,** *proprietors of the boarding house* . . . These lively ladies, twins who are both widowed, are competitive to a fault—who bakes the lightest biscuits? Whose husband was worse? Who can say the most eloquent and (to their boarders' chagrin) the longest grace? And who is the better matchmaker? They'll do almost anything to outdo each other—and absolutely everything to bring loving hearts together!

**JAKE SUTHERLAND,** *the blacksmith* . . . Amidst the workings of his livery stable, he feels right at home. But when it comes to talking to a lady, Jake is awkward, tongue-tied . . . and positively timid!

**JANE CARSON,** *the dressmaker* . . . She wanted to be a doctor like her grandfather. But the eccentric old man decided that wasn't a ladylike career—and bought her a dress shop. Jane named it in his honor: You Sew and Sew. She can sew anything, but she'd rather stitch a wound than a hem.

**ALEXANDER EVANS,** *the newspaperman* . . . He runs *The Harmony Sentinel* with his daughter, Samantha. It took an accident at his press to show Alexander that even a solitary newsman needs love and caring—and he found it in the arms of his lovely bride, Jane Carson.

**JAMES AND LILLIAN TAYLOR,** *owners of the mercantile and post office* . . . With their six children, they're Harmony's wealthiest and most prolific family. It was Lily who acquired the brightly colored paints that brightened the town as part of the Beautification Committee.

**"LUSCIOUS" LOTTIE McGEE,** *owner of "The First Resort"* . . . Lottie's girls sing and dance and even entertain upstairs . . . but Lottie herself is the main attraction at her enticing saloon. And when it comes to taking care of her own niece, this enticing madam is all maternal instinct.

**CORD SPENCER,** *owner of "The Last Resort"* . . . Things sometimes get out of hand at Spencer's rowdy tavern, but he's mostly a good-natured scoundrel who doesn't mean any harm. And when push comes to shove, he'd be the first to put his life on the line for a friend.

**SHERIFF TRAVIS MILLER,** *the lawman* . . . The townsfolk don't always like the way he bends the law a bit when the saloons need a little straightening up. But Travis Miller listens to only one thing when it comes to deciding on the law: his conscience.

**ZEKE GALLAGHER,** *the barber and the dentist* . . . When he doesn't have his nose in a dime Western, the white-whiskered, blue-eyed Zeke is probably making up stories of his own—*or* flirting with the ladies. But not all his tales are just talk—once he really *was* a notorious gunfighter . . .

## A TOWN CALLED HARMONY

Delightful tales that capture the heart of
a small Kansas town—and a simple time when love
was a gift to cherish . . .

*KEEPING FAITH*
by Kathleen Kane

*TAKING CHANCES*
by Rebecca Hagan Lee

*CHASING RAINBOWS*
by Linda Shertzer

*PASSING FANCY*
by Lydia Browne

*PLAYING CUPID*
by Donna Fletcher

*COMING HOME*
by Kathleen Kane

*GETTING HITCHED*
by Ann Justice

*HOLDING HANDS*
by Jo Anne Cassity

*AMAZING GRACE*
by Deborah James

## A TOWN CALLED
## HARMONY

# AMAZING
# GRACE

## Deborah James

DIAMOND BOOKS, NEW YORK

This book is a Diamond original edition,
and has never been previously published.

AMAZING GRACE

A Diamond Book/published by arrangement with
the author

PRINTING HISTORY
Diamond edition/March 1995

ISBN: 0-7865-0080-8

Diamond Books are published by The Berkley Publishing Group,
200 Madison Avenue, New York, NY 10016.
DIAMOND and the "D" design are
trademarks belonging to Charter Communications, Inc.

PRINTED IN THE UNITED STATES OF AMERICA

10  9  8  7  6  5  4  3  2  1

♥
♥ *Prologue*

"MIGHTY FINE CAKE, Maisie." Zeke Gallagher tugged on his belt and pushed his chair away from the big table of the boardinghouse.

Maisie gave her sister a triumphant smile. She'd just earned a point in the twin sisters' endless competition for Zeke's attention. Not that either would know what to do if the roly-poly, twinkly eyed man ever took a real shine to one of them. They loved the competition for its own sake.

"Wipe that grin off your face, Sister. Anyone who eats that icing's goin' to be needin' a trip to Zeke's dentist's chair. That's why he thinks your cake's so all-fired fine. How much sugar did you use, anyway?"

"Just 'cause I'm not stingy like some people," Minnie retorted. "That lemonade of yours could

1

use a little more sugar if you ask me. My lips are going to be puckered for a month of Sundays."

Zeke gave a loud cough that sounded suspiciously like a laugh and both sisters glared at him.

"Speakin' of Sundays," Maisie said. "I've been thinkin' about that new minister of ours. I think he's been lookin' a mite lonely. So I've just written Rebecca Ellen Russell to come for a nice long visit. She knows her Bible verses like a hen knows eggs. I 'spect she'd make a right good Sunday school teacher."

Minnie knocked her glass of lemonade onto Zeke's lap. "You never! Well, you might have told me. I've already sent for Ruth Alice Orndorff. She sings just like an angel straight from heaven. The church choir needs a soloist and they couldn't find one with a purtier voice. She's on her way."

Zeke looked from one sister to the other. It was going to be an interestin' few months, he could see that. A little devil climbed onto Zeke's shoulder and started whispering in his ear.

"I think I'll try my hand at this matchmakin' you two are so fond of. My niece DeeDee is as sweet as your chocolate icing, Maisie. And as sharp as your lemonade, Minnie. I think she'd suit the preacher just fine."

He stood up and tipped his hat. "Excuse me, ladies. I have to go send a telegram."

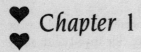

# Chapter 1

Harmony, Kansas
Early Summer, 1874

AT LAST DEEDEE Gallagher was escaping her father's stern, ministerial hand. She suppressed the bubble of freedom's laughter threatening to gush from her throat.

If only the pious Reverend Aaron Gallagher could see her dressed as she was now. How shocked he would be. He had never tolerated her so much as talking about the western costumes worn by the frontier men and women in her books. He would have been outraged to learn that she had actually fashioned an imitation of such garments for herself.

DeeDee chuckled. She had caused quite a com-

motion just outside of St. Louis when she reentered
the riding car from her sleeping berth clad in one of
the buckskin outfits she had brought with her.

Like her father, apparently her fellow travelers
had not been privy to *proper western attire* as was
she. They had ogled her with more than an ample
amount of raised brows, hand-hidden titters, and
gaping mouths. Even the more rough-looking male
journeyers had eyed her with scrunched expressions of dismay.

But why were they so astonished? And why were
none of them dressed as she? She toyed with some
of the fringe dangling from her jacket sleeve. Some
of the people on the train spoke as if they had lived
out West for a good period of time.

Maybe they were simply remaining in keeping
with eastern codes. She shrugged. No matter. *She*
was certainly not going to find herself in an embar-
rassing situation with the Harmony locals upon
her arrival. She had worked hard to make the garments, fashioning them to resemble those she had
seen in the sketches in her penny dredful novels
without either of her parents' knowledge—and by
Heaven, she was determined to wear them.

She smiled thoughtfully and sighed. The women
of her books were daring women to model one-
self after.

Pulling herself back into the present again, she
blinked. Though privy to the unique customs of the
West, DeeDee did not wish to draw any more attention to herself than she already had. After the way
people had reacted to her clothing, what would they

think about the contents of her daydreaming? Even though her mother and father had never known what she was thinking for certain, they had *never* approved.

"Idle hands spark the Devil's attention, Delilah," they had always said. But DeeDee suspected it was much more than *idle hands* that her parents feared— especially her father. He hated her novels, and when he had found the few that she had, he had given her a severe tongue-lashing.

"There are plenty of stories in the Bible if reading is what you wish to do with your free time. Plenty of heroes and heroines, as well, for you to mold yourself after."

DeeDee shivered in the wake of that memory. It was control Reverend Gallagher wanted from his parish members—not to mention his daughter. And he would tolerate nothing short of complete and utter rule over them. Though it was most definitely an exaggeration, to DeeDee's way of thinking, the parishioners could not so much as visit the outhouse without seeking the great wisdom of Aaron Gallagher. Why, it might be a sin if they were to use a page from the Sears, Roebuck catalogue that illustrated a desire as opposed to a need or essential.

Shocked by her own bold thoughts, she darted a quick look around the interior of the swaying railcar at the surrounding passengers. Except for the slight jostling of heads, all appeared to be lost within the realms of their own musings.

She relaxed again, and a joyous prayer skipped

through her mind. *Thank You so much, Lord.* Returning her attention to the open sprawl of the rolling plains racing past her window, she absently thrummed the pages of the small paperback lying in her lap. *Thank You for nudging Uncle Zeke into convincing Father to let me come and stay with him for a summer visit.*

She felt the steady vibration of the train carrying her farther away from the grimy and humdrum city life she had endured for nineteen long years toward what she felt certain was the fresh and exciting existence she had always been destined for. "Harmony," she murmured with a smile. Even the name of the Kansas frontier town beckoned her. Yes, she was finally escaping.

She glanced down at the two books lying atop her knees—one, the Holy Scriptures; the second, *Beadle's Collection of Dime Novels.* Her *textbook* of adventure. Both, in DeeDee's opinion, were words and codes to live by. Though the books were usually in direct conflict with each other, DeeDee managed to see the parallels.

She straightened her posture and tilted her head back and forth. How was a high-spirited, imaginative young woman, a preacher's daughter raised within the cloistered boundaries of a strict Methodist upbringing, supposed to expose herself to the glorious wonders of the world waiting just beyond the urban streets of Dallas, Pennsylvania? Why, wonderfully written adventures of the West, of course. There one could be certain to find the factual truth of the Western wilds.

Remembering the many lectures she had received from her father, she sighed with a triumphant arch of one brow. What could he possibly know about the malleable ethics or loose morals depicted in the *fictitious, half-told yarns*, as he was inclined to call them? He had never been any farther west than his own Dallas parish.

Feeling a twinge of guilt for her thoughts, DeeDee quickly sought a distraction. She could not—would not—allow any pangs of self-condemnation to spoil her trip. Especially not now, when she was only a few miles from Harmony, and a whole summer of adventures with her uncle.

She flipped the pages open to the spot where she had been reading earlier. With an admiring hand, she traced the drawing of the hard-faced, only slightly feminine figure staring out from the paper. She began to read where she had stopped.

Bang! Bang! Bang! Bang! Four shots rang out on the midnight air!

"Git outta here, Sue. This ain't yer fight. These Injuns mean business." Sternly arose the white man's shout amid the blazing of guns and the whizzing of tomahawks as they flashed through the air on their message of blood.

"What, an' let ya have all the fun?" Above the outburst of the war-whoop of the savages, Sue grinned, despite the scene of impending slaughter. She lifted her brace of revolvers and pulled back the hammers. "Ain't nothin' I enjoy more'n a good tussle. I'm in it to the end."

Many a dusky, painted form bit the dust, and many a savage howl followed the discharge of the guns aimed at them. On and on, heart to heart, muzzle to muzzle, the white man and woman battled together.

The trees above them drooped under a cloud of smoke, and their trunks were scarred with gashes, cut by the tomahawks which had missed their more deadly aim. The ground was burdened with the red man's dead, until at last, all lay still in a frozen stare of death.

DeeDee's heart hammered against her chest. What a dashing adventure. She could not read fast enough to keep up with the rush of excitement the story provoked within her.

With wild sardonic laughter, the man called Deadwood Sam arose, his small gang of road-riders slowly joining his side. Lowering his still-smoking rifle, Sam turned to his longtime love, his dark eyes gleaming with intense bloodlust.

Standing slowly, Sue met him with a mirrored stare. Clothed in a tight-fitting habit of buckskin, she looked to be at an age somewhere between sixteen and twenty, trim, and compactly built with a preponderance of muscular curves and an animal spirit; square, iron-cast shoulders; limbs small yet like bars of steel; and with a grace of position in the saddle rarely equaled; she made a fine picture for an artist's brush or a poet's pen.

Sam grabbed her, yanking her hard against

him. "Marry me, Susie," he asked for what must have been the hundredth time, his voice drawn on the exhilarated pants of his breathing.

Daringly, she lifted a brow and laughed out loud. "Ya know there ain't no man fer me but Steele, an' I ain't even so sure 'bout him." She shoved Sam roughly away, thrust her pistols back into their holsters, then wheeled toward her horse waiting nearby. Leaping into the saddle, she sent him the taunt of a challenging smile, amusement flashing in her eyes. "But don't stop askin'." Then, with a nod toward the sprawl of dead savages, she wheeled her mount down the road toward the Dakotas. She raised her hand in a backward wave. "Obliged fer the frolic, boys! See ya in Hell if not before!"

The train's whistle screeched above the steady clatter and drone of its metal wheels.

Startled, DeeDee sucked in a rush of air. Blinking, she peered out through the sun-drenched pane of glass beside her. She could not wait to set foot in Harmony. What glorious adventure waited for her there? She shot a glance downward, before returning her stare out the window. And romance? Would she be as lucky as her heroines? Would she find a real live hero to love? If so, would he love her back?

Clasping the novel to her chest, she embraced the book as if it were an unseen lover. She sighed. Oh, yes, Lord, someone just like big Jim Steele.

The train announced its presence again.

Lowering the book back to her lap, DeeDee

focused on the scenery outside the glass. They were beginning to slow down. Were they already to Harmony? Her heartbeat quickened with anticipation. Scooting closer to the window, she looked from side to side, filling her gaze with the midafternoon sights.

The rolling ocean of grassland had suddenly been dotted with tranquil homesteads. A few trees appeared, and on the opposite side of a gleaming expanse of a river, some farm animals came into view. In the distance children waved from their various chores or dallyings.

Farms? Disappointment tweaked DeeDee's soul. They were not much different from the homesteads on the outskirts of Dallas. Where was all of the hurly-burly she had been promised in Beadle's portrayal of the Wild West?

*This* is *just the surrounding area.* She wet her lips expectantly. Surely the town itself would fairly ooze with a noteworthy atmosphere of rugged beauty, stimulating activity, and outrageous rascals.

Brightly painted buildings suddenly moved in on her vision.

"Harmony—Harmony, Kansas, folks," the conductor called out from behind her in the unfaltering, impersonal voice she had grown accustomed to hearing over the last two weeks.

The repeating toot of the train whistle caused DeeDee's insides to tighten. She was finally here! Her life was finally about to begin! Adrenaline pumping, she slapped the book closed, then shoved it, along with her Bible, into the gaping mouth of her personal satchel lying at her feet.

Taking one last look out the window, she pushed back her bangs from her eyes and tugged down the small bill of her regulation army kepi more securely on her head. She started to rise.

"Please, *wait* till the Number Five has pulled up to a complete stop before standing," the doleful-faced conductor bellowed. Holding on to the back of DeeDee's seat, he cut her what appeared to be a tolerant look, then braced himself against the pitch of the slowing train.

Following his order, DeeDee plopped herself back down on the wooden bench. Normally she would have begged pardon for her actions and lowered her gaze demurely, but that was not a social necessity out here. And since she was now *officially* in the West, she might as well start enjoying some of the outlandish practices accepted in a woman in this gruff and blunt territory.

She lifted her chin, snubbing the man, before returning her attention to the small crowd now awaiting the train on the station platform. She ran her gaze over the various faces. None was familiar. Where was Uncle Zeke? Had he not come to meet her?

The railcar lurched to a full stop.

"Harmony, Kansas," the fare collector called out again. "For those of you goin' on to Wichita and Dodge City, we'll be here 'bout an hour takin' on fuel and water."

An excited rush of voices arose.

DeeDee was so elated she could hardly control the impulse to leap up with a shout of joy. Snatching the handle of her bag, she jumped to her feet. She started to push her way into the line of passengers forming down the middle of the aisle, but, seeing an older woman blocking her path, DeeDee respectfully smiled and let the woman go by.

Crowned with a smartly fashioned bonnet of pheasant feathers and colorful blossoms accenting her jade corduroy traveling suit, the matron gave a cordial smile. But as her gaze swept downward over DeeDee's rustic appearance, the smile drooped to a disapproving pucker. Clutching her oversize reticule beneath her sagging bosom, the woman snubbed DeeDee with a curt upswing of her chin.

One long plume batted DeeDee's cheek.

Tensing, she balled her fists. She should clout the old hag for that impolite display. But, much as she would like to act the part of the frontier female, DeeDee had not, as yet, been able to completely push aside her civil upbringing. But that time would come—at least, she hoped so. She hated the thought of being a milksop forever, ready to do another's bidding just because it was expected.

Once everyone had disembarked from the train, DeeDee took a deep breath and moved to the doorway overlooking the station deck.

Most of the passengers were ambling into the center of town, and on to their prospective destinations. But Uncle Zeke was nowhere to be found. What had happened? Had he forgotten that she was due in today? Father *had* wired him of the date of her arrival. She peered around at the self-absorbed expressions of the people milling about the town. So where was Uncle Zeke?

She swept a critical gaze over the main street. And where was all the frenzy of excitement she had been led to believe would be cycloning within the town? It seemed Harmony, Kansas, was just that, tranquil and—

She caught the sound of water splashing off to the side of her. Turning, she saw what must be the town mill. Watching the huge paddle wheel turn, she sighed. *Oh, Lord, help me.* Harmony appeared to be as boring as her own town of Dallas.

"You need some help, uh, ma'am?" the conductor asked from close behind her.

Clutching the doorframe with one hand, DeeDee cut a startled look over her shoulder.

After ransacking her with what DeeDee considered an all-too-critical inspection, the man lifted a questioning brow.

Whether he was simply curious about her welfare or objected to her semi-masculine attire, DeeDee was unsure. She felt a sting of irritation, though she was not certain why.

"'Scuse me." He nodded toward the station. "But if there's nothin' I can do for you, *ma'am,* I got important business to tend to."

"Important?" she asked. Was he implying that *she* was not important? She did not like the way he used the word *ma'am,* either. Did the man think that she was such a tenderfoot that she would tolerate his rudeness? Her first test. Maybe she could find some excitement after all.

Was he—what did they call it out here?—oh, yes, *brewin' fer trouble?* She drew herself up rigid. "And just what do—" She halted mid-thought. Oh, no, this would never do. If she was going to enjoy this frontier adventure to its fullest, she would have to put her western knowledge to use, starting with the language.

Squinting at him, she looked him up and down. His less than threatening physique bolstered her naive eagerness. In search of a more confident posture, she shifted her feet slightly apart, then cleared her throat with an unladylike sound. "Jist what'd ya mean b'that, mister?"

Frowning, the man pulled back a little and stared at her as if she had spoken in a foreign tongue. Apparently regaining his thoughts, he sighed. "Yer pardon, ma'am. I wasn't tryin' to be nosy. It's my job to see that the passengers are taken care of properly."

DeeDee blinked. Had she misread the man's inquiry?

"And, well, I just assumed that since nobody was here to meet you—well, I—" He darted a glance past her again, before meeting her with another puzzled but stern look. "Is there anywhere I can direct you?"

DeeDee felt her arrogance take a swift departure. She had just reacted as her father would have—something she detested. She had gained control over another by bullying. She flinched inwardly. She had read *this* scene completely wrong. "I beg your pardon, sir. I misunderstood your intentions."

He smiled tolerantly, flashing a row of discolored dentures of poor quality. "No problem, ma'am."

She turned back toward the open air and stepped down to the platform. "Actually," she said, hoping to hurry beyond her mistake, "could you tell me where to locate the barbershop?"

"Barbershop?" He ran a surprised glance over her garments again.

"Yes." Turning to face him, DeeDee gripped the handle of her satchel tighter, but held her temper in check. He was studying her with that strange look again. "It's my uncle's. He owns it."

"Zeke Gallagher's your uncle?"

"Why, yes." Now what? Did the man believe that her choice of clothing prohibited her from having such a relative?

The conductor snorted a chuckle. "The man's just full of surprises."

"You know him?"

"Sure do." The rail-thin man spread his lips wide. "I live here in Harmony when I'm not on duty with the train. Zeke's a good friend of mine. Fixed me up with these choppers here until my new ones are delivered from back East." His grin broadened. "They'll be real porcelain."

DeeDee's brows shot upward. She had forgotten that her uncle was also the resident dentist. Watching the man's prideful expression, she had to hold back a grin. "How wonderful for you."

"Ain't it, though?" He stepped down from the train exit. "That Zeke, he stays up on the latest stuff, you know. You gotta mouth problem, or just want a good shave or haircut, well, sir, he's the one to go to." He winked. "Knows everything that's goin' on in town, too."

"Really?"

The conductor nodded, then pointed around the side of the depot. "Cut down through there, and you'll come to the main street. You'll see a green building. That's Zeke's business. Cain't miss it."

DeeDee smiled. She took a step in the direction he had indicated, but stopped short. She looked back. "Oh, I forgot my luggage."

The man waved her off. "I'll have it held for you in the depot. How many?"

"Two. They're marked with the name Gallagher."

He nodded, then wheeled away and headed down the tracks toward the end of the train. "I'll find 'em."

Well, Harmony might not be wild and lively, as she had hoped, but at least the people seemed friendly enough here. With a brisk stride, she crossed the planked walk, then cut around the depot as the conductor had instructed.

She breathed in the warm air and shrugged. Now to find Uncle Zeke. Thrilled to finally be here, she hurried her step.

Zeke Gallagher had only come back to Dallas on three rare occasions, once when she was real little and sick with the chicken pox, another time a few years later when he had stopped off from what he had called a business trip, and again three years ago for her sixteenth birthday when her mother had given her a "coming-out" party.

Scuffing her heels against the hard-packed dirt, she snorted to herself. Coming-out party. She had hated it. All those frilly-dilly girls in their frilly-dilly dresses. She shuddered. And her mother had made her wear the frilliest, dilliest gown of all.

Remembering the silky texture of the soft lace gown, and the way her mother had smiled at her when DeeDee had put it on, she sighed reluctantly. It really had not been *that* awful wearing the dress. She would never admit it out loud, but she had rather liked the soft, feminine feel of the gown. It was one of the very few times she had actually felt pretty. It was the one time she could ever remember her mother doing anything that was not overseen by her father.

Aaron Gallagher was not keen on vanity. In his opinion DeeDee needed nothing more than a plain, simple dress—anything else was extravagant and boastful. The Reverend Gallagher was not keen on much of anything that made a person feel prideful or made one feel any amount of self-worth. "Pride and vanity are the Devil's tools!" he would bellow with an uplifted fist whenever he caught her glancing in the small hall rack mirror of their home.

DeeDee rolled her eyes. *So whose tool is the big looking glass in the attic that Father always stands in front of whenever he practices his sermons?* she thought. *I doubt the Lord cares how attractive or well-proportioned his servants are when they deliver his word to the people. Hmph! Father's just as prideful as anyone else—he just hides it better than most.*

Entering upon what must have been Harmony's Main Street, DeeDee turned her attention to the different businesses. Purple? Pink? The buildings were all painted in bright shades. She gaped, her eyes darting from color to color. Then she caught sight of a green building with a pole striped like a candy cane in front of it. Uncle Zeke's!

She hurried across the roadway, dodging buggies and pedestrians alike. She could hardly wait to see him. It had been so long, and he was so much fun. Besides the new dress her mother had made for her, *he* had been the single enjoyment of that birthday party. When he had discovered how unhappy she had been at the celebration, Uncle Zeke had taken her fishing. Fishing! And in that expensive frilly lavender dress, too.

He always did know how to have fun and make her laugh. And *he* did not have a problem with her reading her dime novels. In fact, it was a passion they shared. Uncle Zeke had been the one to get her started with them when she was twelve. He had always been her favorite relative, and she loved him more than anyone. He had been a gunman and really had adventures. So many that when he moved to Harmony, he had changed his last name to Gallagher. It was the first name he thought of, since it was his brother-in-law's. Besides, he always told her, a minister's good name might not be all bad. He always told her he liked Harmony and didn't mind that his days on the move were behind him.

"Look at that," a youthful voice called out above the noises of the town.

DeeDee glanced to one side toward two teenage youths. They looked to be only a few years younger than she.

"Ya think that's a gal or a fella?" the boy with black hair called out to his taller friend. His tone rang louder than necessary.

The blond folded his arms and shrugged, then took a step toward her. "Heck, Billy, it's got to be a fella. It's goin' into the barbershop, ain't it?"

DeeDee slowed her pace. She looked around wondering who they were talking about. Seeing no one, she peered back at them. Apparently, they were directing their conversation to her and her attire. She stopped short in front of the watering trough outside the shop.

Here was her chance to show some real western bravado. Narrowing her eyes, she turned to face them fully. Well, she *had* wanted a little excitement. "You boys talkin' 'bout me?"

The youths approached, both with smug, taunting expressions.

"Well, Red, I s'pose we was," the arrogant blond said.

DeeDee stiffened. Now what? She moved to keep them both in full view, but the dark-haired boy called Billy eased around behind her. "What can I do for you?" she asked as sternly as she could muster. In truth she felt more than a little nervous.

"You can settle an argument for us." The taller boy facing her pulled on a lengthy lock of her auburn hair.

She snatched it out of his grasp. "I wouldn't do that if I were you." She tried to force the fear from her voice, but it trembled despite her effort. She straddled her feet apart, bracing herself for trouble as the characters in Beadle's were sometimes said to do.

"Or what?"

"Yeah," the boy behind her added.

"We jist wanna know if'n yore a fella or a gal s'all." The blond reached for her hair again. "Ain't never seen a fella with such long, purty red hair b'fore."

"I'm a girl," DeeDee said between clenched teeth. Her anger was slowly exceeding her fear. She swallowed.

"In britches?" Billy shrieked close to her back.

"I ain't never seen no gal in britches like *those* b'fore."

"Uh-uh, me, neither."

DeeDee felt the kid behind her pluck boldly at the fringes dangling from one hip. She jerked around. "Don't!" True fear gripped her senses. What did these boys want with her? And what was she suppose to do now? Her dime novel heroines never got kidded because of what they wore. Her pulse quickened. She could not think straight, she was so stunned by the boys' attack. Why could she not do this? All of her earlier bravado fled. She peered up and down the street in search of anyone who might come to her aid.

*Well*, she told herself, *this* is *just the kind of adventure you wanted, so . . .* She swallowed again, trying desperately to calm the racing of her heart. So, now what? She cut a glance over her shoulder toward the barbershop. *Uncle Zeke, where are you?* But there was no sign of him. She would have to handle this alone.

She thought of the story she had just read, and how Sue had handled Deadwood Sam. The frontier woman had been able to easily manage the situation in that adventure. But this was not a tale in Beadle's, and neither of these two were in love with her as Deadwood was with Sue. No. This predicament would take more force than that.

Could she resolve it as assuredly as Sue had? She had no choice but to be vehement in her conviction. Squaring her shoulders, she gripped the handle on her satchel tighter. She had to try. "If either of you so much as—"

"Hey, there!" A scuffling of footsteps sounded behind her. A hand touched her shoulder. "Are you—"

Quick to react, DeeDee whirled around. She swung her bag into her attacker's face.

With a loud splash he fell into the watering trough.

"I told you not to touch me!"

The blond roared with laughter, and a crowd began to gather.

Lifting her gaze, DeeDee's eyes flew wide.

Stumbling in a fit of hilarity in front of her stood the dark-haired boy.

Her stomach tightened. Shocked, she shot a horrified look at the trough. If Billy was pitching back and forth in front of the barbershop, cackling, then who had she knocked into the water?

Only a pair of masculine hands and Creedmore shoes like the ones her father wore were visible above the water.

She rushed forward. "I'm sorry, mister," she wailed. Reaching down, she grasped hold of a flailing wrist and pulled. "I thought you were—" Determined to undo her folly, she leaned forward, and tugged harder.

The man surfaced with a sputter.

"Hold on there!" Heavy footsteps charged toward her.

Someone grabbed her arm and spun her around.

DeeDee flinched, blinked, then focused on the cool blue eyes of her uncle.

"Why, DeeDee, girl," he said with that all-too-familiar, deep-throated chuckle she had always loved. "You're here!"

DeeDee blinked. "Uncle Zeke." Mouth agape, she nodded, then darted her gaze back to the drenched man.

Zeke Gallagher grasped hold of the man's soggy arm. "It *is* a might warm today, Reverend."

Reverend? DeeDee cringed. Holding on to a breath, she sought out the face below hers. Her gaze riveted on the stiff white collar encircling the man's neck. Her hand flew to her mouth. "Oh, no, please," she murmured. "Not that."

Zeke steadied the man. "Don't ya think ya'd enjoy a dip in the swimmin' pond a bunch better'n this?"

Uproarious laughter from the spectators followed her uncle's quip.

DeeDee's face flamed hot with humiliation. In her intempered haste, she had not looked before she reacted, and now it seemed she had knocked the town minister into the watering trough. She squeezed her eyes closed and swallowed with a discernable gulp. *Oh, my good Lord in Heaven. What have I done?*

♥ **Chapter 2**
♥

SPRAWLED IN THE overflowing trough in front of the barbershop, Joshua Wylie lifted a confused stare to the strange girl wavering above him dressed in masculine garb. What had he done to provoke such an unwarranted attack from her? He had only meant to aid her in her predicament with those mischievous boys.

"Parson?"

Joshua shifted his attention to the man holding on to his forearm. He blinked the water from his eyes.

"You want outta there anytime soon?" Zeke Gallagher grinned down at him. A flash of the barber's white teeth gleamed from beneath an even whiter bushy beard.

25

After darting a still perplexed look down at the glistening liquid engulfing him, then up at the girl again, Joshua finally returned his gaze to the whiskered man. He clutched Zeke's upper arm more securely. "Yes—yes, of course—the trough," he said, stumbling over his reply as he was hoisted unceremoniously out of the box.

"Oh, please forgive me," the young lady said, the eloquence of her voice belying the primitive cut of her clothing.

"That's quite all right, my dear." Joshua offered her a reassuring smile while shaking the water from his pants legs.

"No, really, it was all my fault. I—uh—" She looked up at him, her soft blue eyes displaying a look of true remorse beneath her brow-length auburn bangs. "I thought you were one of them." She shot a glare at the still snickering teenagers.

In the three short weeks since he had first arrived to take over as Harmony's new minister from Reverend Johnson, Joshua had come to a hasty conclusion that *those* two boys were definitely the parish mischiefs—especially Billy Taylor. It seemed that even though he was basically a good kid, the boy was forever getting into trouble in some way or another. He always claimed that, whatever the commotion, he had good cause—the gossip column he wrote in *The Harmony Sentinel*. Today was no exception.

Joshua returned his attention to the girl. "Believe me, I do understand, Miss—um—" Forgetting his soggy attire a moment, he peered harder at her. Who was she? Small as Harmony was, he thought he had been introduced to just about the entire populace. How was it now that he had never met this attractive, yet peculiar, young lady? Surely he would remember her.

"I say, beg pardon, Parson," Zeke interrupted with a snap of his fingers. He pulled the girl up to stand closer in front of Joshua. "This here's my—my—niece. Yeah, Delilah Gallagher—DeeDee for short. Come all the way out from Dallas, Pennsylvania, to spend the summer with me." He gave her a quick hug.

A rustle of shocked murmurs flew from the spectators.

"Delilah!" a prim and proper young woman with perfectly curled blonde hair exclaimed. "Did you hear that?"

"A hussy's name," her companion spouted.

Rage instantly marked DeeDee's face red. She whirled around.

Her overstuffed satchel caught Joshua off guard, slamming into his knees. Thrown off balance, he stumbled back. Too late, he felt the side of the trough. He teetered backward. He groped for anything solid, but only caught air. Bottom first, he plunged into the narrow box with a loud splash.

Like a sword thrust into the heart of its foe, a deadly silence slashed through the gathered crowd . . . but only for one breathless second. For in the next instant, a roar of laughter attacked Joshua's hearing.

Embarrassment, anger, and confusion assaulted his senses. The girl had done it to him again! He floundered in the water a moment before hoisting himself upright.

Delilah Gallagher wheeled around to face him. Eyes rounded, her hand flew to her mouth. "Not again! Oh, here, please." She reached out and clasped hold of his wrist. "Let me help you."

Unable to keep his anger in check, Joshua gave in to the emotion. He jerked out of her grasp. "No!" He could do without *her* kind of help. Had not one dunking been enough for her?

She flinched, and took a step back.

He grabbed the sides of the trough.

"Come on, now." Zeke grasped Joshua's arm and yanked him up. "DeeDee was just tryin' to apologize. It wasn't like she meant to drown you or nothin'." He chuckled.

The gatherers seemed to hang on an apprehensive breath. No one spoke.

Looking at his parishioners, Joshua slowly inhaled. What a well-painted picture of Christian love he must pose right now . . . the new minister rejecting one of his own congregation. *This*, he was quite certain, was not what Reverend Terrance Harkington, his mentor, and the only father figure Joshua had ever known, had meant by, *"Let your flock come to know the spirit within you, and they will surely gather unto your embrace."* Joshua turned his attention from the townspeople to the girl.

Zeke moved around to stand behind his niece, his hands clutching her shoulders protectively, a solid scowl challenging Joshua.

"Forgive me, Miss Gallagher. It wasn't my intention to sound so harsh."

Zeke appeared to relax.

The girl did not. The hostility that flashed within her still-battle-lighted eyes was enough to thwart the most stout-hearted soldier. "It *was* an accident," she stated indignantly. Securing the handle of her satchel tighter in her grasp, she peered up at her uncle. "Boy, this town's about as friendly as— as—" She seemed to be at a loss for just the proper description. "As a pack of howlin' Injuns."

Zeke chuckled, causing his sizable girth to bounce. "Injuns?" He shook his head, and gently squeezed her shoulders like a beloved accordion. "You gotta stop spendin' so much time readin' them novels I've been sendin' you."

The crowd, deciding their preacher had taken his last dunking, began to break up. Novels? Joshua could not imagine what reading stories had to do with the girl's remark. Surely Zeke could not truly be objecting to his niece having an education. So far, it seemed to be the one and only positive attribute possessed by the young lady.

Stepping around the girl, Zeke retrieved Joshua's soggy hat, still floating in the water, and handed the drenched headdress to him.

Joshua accepted his hat with all the graciousness he could muster.

Further down Main Street, Samantha Spencer and Faith Kincaid stepped out of Jane Carson's You Sew and Sew shop, and saw Joshua still shaking water off himself as he headed toward the boardinghouse.

"What on earth could have happened?" Faith asked.

"I don't know, but Zeke should be leading that young lady to Jane's instead of his barbershop. She looks like she stepped out of one of his novels," Sam replied. "But she looks like she'll liven up Harmony. I guess she's Zeke's niece. Remember, we heard she was coming to town. I hope we meet her soon."

A couple hours later, in his room at the boarding-house, Joshua stood in front of the mirrored doors of his wardrobe closet, straightening his white linen collar. Minnie had come by earlier and taken his suit to be washed, dried, and pressed. After the dunking he'd just experienced, though, the suit could probably do without the washing.

"Reverend," Maisie hollered through the door. "Supper's on the table. Better come down. There's nothing worse than Minnie's cookin'. Except Minnie's cookin' cold."

"I heard that, Sister," Minnie called up the stairs.

"'Spected you did," Maisie called back.

"Yes, ma'am." Joshua sighed. He wasn't looking forward to another evening of the sisters' match-making. Last night Maisie had asked Ruth Alice to recite all the books of the Bible—forward and backward.

Then Minnie forced Rebecca to sing what he had to believe was every hymn she knew.

His jaws ached so much from smiling he could hardly eat breakfast the next morning. It wasn't that both young women didn't have their fine points.

But if and when Joshua decided to take a wife, he wanted to do the choosing himself.

Staring at his well-groomed reflection, Joshua listened to the clip-clop of Maisie's oxford heels retreating down the hall. He felt a pinch on the back of his neck where his collar buttoned. He slid his finger between the stiff linen and his skin and smoothed the inside edge, trying to make it comfortable.

He'd waited so long to earn a collar, yet now that it was part of his proper attire, he didn't care much for it. The rigid material always chafed his neck.

Briefly he contemplated not wearing it to supper. He frowned at the red mark half-circling his throat. Why was it so important that a man of the cloth don the band? Did it truly change the man? He sighed. *Why fight it, Josh ol' boy?* It just would not be proper to be seen without it.

"Reverend, we're going to have to feed your supper to the hogs if you don't get yourself down here." Was it Maisie or Minnie yelling up the stairs? Sometimes Josh couldn't tell the twins' voices apart.

Resigning himself to the inescapable, he crossed the room and sat on the side of the bed. He slipped his feet inside his shoes and grimaced, curling his toes against the damp leather. He thought about his old work boots in the wardrobe, but shook his head. No. He bent down, pulled the laces up tight, and tied them. Work boots, dry and comfortable as they might be, would not be *proper* to wear to supper. A minister must be proper.

Joshua's shoes creaked as he made his way to the dining room. He stopped outside the door. How was he going to get to the table without someone noticing the sodden squeak?

He glared down at the wet Creedmores as if they were a loathsome informant. Everyone knew of Joshua's afternoon exploits, but must it be announced so blatantly? He lifted his eyes heavenward. "Lord, grant me humility," he murmured.

*If this is the only humiliation you should ever suffer, Joshua, count your blessings*, came the response from within.

He closed his eyes with a groan. He could not argue with that. But then, he never argued with anyone, about anything. He thought of Reverend Harkington. Lord, how he would love to be more like that man. Even now, at seventy-two, the man was anything but passive.

He had thoroughly executed his will over the children at the Syracuse orphanage where Joshua had grown up in New York. He was known to be cunningly influential—forcefully so at times and flagrantly manipulative when the occasion called for more drastic measures. Joshua shook his head. But never *passive*.

But Joshua was not Reverend Harkington. And even though it went against the grain, Joshua had found that being humble and obedient was the only way he could handle living at the orphanage. He had been an outcast for so long that this behavior had become second nature.

He took a deep breath and marched into the dining room. With each step, his shoes declared their soggy torment. Halting mid-stride, he shot a look at the twin ladies.

Mirror images of each other, two sets of blue eyes darted looks at his feet.

He knew nothing would give them greater pleasure than to discover something—anything—extra to add to the story of the confrontation in front of the barbershop. It would make for wonderful conversation at the next Ladies' Auxiliary meeting.

Joshua gritted his teeth, then relaxed, deciding that playing innocent was the best way to handle this situation. He would act as though nothing out of the ordinary had occurred that day. "Good evening, ladies," he said cordially, nodding to Maisie and Minnie and being careful to smile at Ruth Alice and Rebecca with exactly the same degree of warmth. He was not going to get drawn into the twins' ridiculous matchmaking contest.

"Oh, Reverend," Ruth Alice gushed. "I hope you didn't catch a chill after your ordeal today."

Minnie moved up to stand besided the young blond woman seated opposite Joshua. "Now, Sister, isn't that just like Ruth Alice?" she asked while leaning across the lace-draped table and setting a plate in front of Joshua.

Maisie gave a muffled snort.

Minnie stroked the curls at the back of Ruth Alice's head. "Always concerned about everyone." She gave Joshua a significant look.

To Joshua's way of thinking, Ruth Alice did not need any kind of protectress—even if she was the daughter of Minnie's best childhood friend. The young lady was more than able to show off her own assets. She was always blushing prettily and batting her lashes at him in a way Joshua found a bit too calculating. Although enjoyable to watch.

"Rebecca, why don't you say grace tonight?" Maisie leaped in to champion her own candidate for minister's wife. "Didn't you tell me you wanted to ask the Almighty to make sure the Reverend didn't catch cold?"

Rebecca hesitated, and Joshua could have sworn Maisie gave her a kick under the table.

"Yes, ma'am," Rebecca said obediently, giving Joshua a timid smile. He almost had to feel sorry for the girl being bossed so by Maisie.

Before Rebecca could begin, Zeke Gallagher ambled in and slapped Joshua soundly on the back.

Joshua jumped. "Relax, Parson." He bent nearer to Joshua's ear. "Ain't no watering trough around for a good hun'erd yards or better." He winked, offering Joshua a good-natured chuckle before taking his seat next to the younger man.

"What about your niece?" Joshua teased in a low voice. "How close is she?"

"Liked DeeDee, did you? Well, don't fret none. She'll be down d'rectly. She's staying right here in the boardinghouse." Zeke scooted his chair up closer to the table, then nodded a greeting to the four women.

"Huh-hum."

All eyes turned in the direction of the sound.

Dressed in the same frontier garments as earlier, Delilah Gallagher stood in the doorway of the dining room. Open curiosity added to the lively blue spark twinkling in her large eyes.

Joshua immediately jumped to his feet. Forgetting his manners a moment, he allowed himself an appreciative gaze over the glorious cascade of auburn hair spilling down one shoulder to her waist.

"C'mon in, DeeDee," Zeke said from behind Joshua. "You met Minnie and Maisie already. And I'm sure you remember Reverend Wylie."

DeeDee sat down. "And this here's Miss Ruth Alice Orndorff," Zeke continued. "She's the daughter of some girlhood friend of Minnie's, or somethin' like that. And this other young lady is Miss Rebecca Ellen Russell, who's related somehow or other to Maisie."

"It's too bad you didn't have time to freshen up after your long trip, Delilah, dear," Ruth Alice said.

"Delilah. That's a Biblical name, you know," Rebecca commented. "She was the one who—"

"DeeDee," Zeke emphasized. "No one calls her Delilah."

"Dee . . . Dee," Ruth Alice repeated, tilting her head from side to side. The way she said the name, Joshua had to think it left a bitter taste in her mouth.

Joshua fired a critical look in Ruth Alice's direction. The girl had done nothing to her. Why was she being so unpleasant? He glanced at DeeDee. He noticed the tension in her posture, but she simply smiled at the other two young women.

Minnie peered at Joshua. "Can I get you something, Reverend?"

Startled, he lifted his gaze from DeeDee. He had not realized he was still standing. "Um—no."

Zeke flashed Minnie a triumphant grin. "I'm sure DeeDee appreciates the courtesy, Parson, but there's only us two men between all these womenfolk. We'd darn near starve if we had to keep jumping up and down."

"I think it's refreshing to see a man with *proper* social graces," Ruth Alice commented, simpering at Joshua.

"Hell, my graces are just as good as any man's in town," Zeke burst out. "But if me and the parson took a notion to get up everytime one of you hens goes in or out, why, hell, we'd likely wind up with a severe case of rheumatism before we was to get old."

"Zeke Gallagher!" Maisie all but shouted. "If you don't mind your manners you'll feel my broom to your backside. It'll be worse than any rheumatism, I can tell you. Besides, you're old already."

"Not as old as some," Zeke whispered to Joshua, shaking with silent laughter.

Maisie sent Zeke a bone-chilling glower. Apparently, she had heard his remark. "Rebecca, can we have the blessing, please?"

By the time Rebecca had finished thanking the Almighty for every single blessing the day had brought, and making several pleas for Joshua's good health, supper had cooled considerably.

Minnie jumped right in as soon as the grace was over. "Reverend, Ruth Alice has a solo in the hymn the choir's got planned for this Sunday. Maybe if we ask real nice she'll sing it for us after supper."

Joshua smiled politely.

"Now, Sister," Maisie said. "I was thinking after supper we'd just leave the Reverend and Rebecca alone in the parlor. She's been working hard on her lesson for Sunday school, and I know she'd be right grateful for some advice."

Joshua nodded politely.

"DeeDee here might like to join you," Zeke volunteered. "Doesn't it sound mighty interesting?" He gave his niece a significant look.

"Actually," DeeDee answered, "I want to finish my novel."

"Oh, what are you reading, dear?" Rebecca asked.

Zeke started to shake his head.

"It's called *The Desperado's Darling*," DeeDee replied eagerly. "I'd be happy to loan it to you if you like. It's filled with shoot-outs and fistfights. And saloon girls. That's who the desperado's darling is. She wears this red satin dress up past her knees, and—"

♥
♥ **Chapter 3**

HALF-DRAGGED BY her uncle from the boardinghouse and into the early evening air, DeeDee practically had to run to keep up with him. Why was
he so upset with her? And just what *had* she done
that was so wrong?

"Uncle Zeke, you're hurting me," she said, trying
not to whine, but failing.

He loosened his hold, but did not relinquish his
grasp completely. Taking overly large strides, he
headed up the boardwalk toward the dark green
building of his barbershop.

"Uncle Zeke, what did I do?" DeeDee hurried to
stay in step with his pace. Craning her neck, she
looked up, trying to catch a glimpse of his expression, but the twilight sky did little to aid her effort.

Zeke pulled up short in front of the barbershop

entrance. With his free hand, he fumbled in his pocket, then withdrew a key and unlocked the door. Gently, but firmly, he pushed her ahead of him. Once inside, he closed the door behind them.

Even before DeeDee's eyes had time to adjust to the meager light entering in through the large multipaned front window, the heavy, masculine aroma of bay rum mixed with what she could only assume was wood-violet aftershave attacked her sense of smell. She wriggled her nose against the strong, balmy fragrances.

A flame sparked, and Zeke lit a nearby lamp. His austere expression took aim at her.

On instinct she stepped back, bumping into a counter.

The display case teetered. A glass jar crashed to the planked floor.

Whirling around, DeeDee barely caught a bottle doing its best to follow. She sighed with relief just as the broken shards flickered into view. She tensed, then sent a hesitant glance in her uncle's direction. "I—I'm sorry, Uncle Zeke."

Hands on hips, he looked heavenward and exhaled with an exasperated sound.

Squatting down, DeeDee quickly gathered the wet glass, a jellylike substance sticking to her fingers. "I'll have this cleaned up in a jiff—"

"Oh, DeeDee, girl, what've I gotten myself into?" Zeke moved up next to her.

Quickly she picked up a large piece still sporting a lable.

*Eastman's Genuine Crystal Shampoo Jelly.*

The sickly-sweet perfumed fragrance nearly over-powered her. "Don't worry, Uncle Zeke." She coughed. "I'll pay for it."

He bent down and gripped her by the shoulders. "Leave it, girl."

"But I want to—"

"It ain't a problem." He glanced at the counter, indicating with a nod that she set down the few broken shards she held. "But what just happened back at supper—now, that's a problem."

DeeDee grasped a folded towel from a nearby stack and wiped her hands clean. She shrugged. "Like I said, I really don't understand what all the fuss's about. I was just making conversation."

"That may be but—"

"Boy, that Ruth Alice looks like she ate a bushel of lemons. I guess she's not a dime novel fan." She had to find safer ground to put between them.

Zeke jabbed a finger just beyond her nose. His usual jovial expression appeared taut. "Don't you go tryin' to change the subject, girl."

DeeDee flinched. Never, for as far back as she could recall, had she ever witnessed her mother's brother being even a little cross with anyone, much less truly displeased—and especially never with her. But now, only a few short hours into her visit, she had managed to provoke what appeared to be true anger in him.

Maybe she could coax him to her way of thinking as she had when she had been a child. Swallowing, she mustered her courage, smiled sweetly, and placed her palm to his chest. "Oh, c'mon now, Uncle Zeke. I didn't mean no harm."

He pressed her shoulders tighter between his huge hands, his fingers digging into her skin. "I read those books, too, but I don't tell people about them."

DeeDee trembled, but held on to her resolve. She would not let her uncle see that she was even a little afraid. She thought of her novels, and the heroines, then squared her shoulders. If she was going to truly imitate the frontier women's unflinching demeanor, as she had always dreamed about, she would have to retain complete composure. "All I said was—"

"I know what you said." Zeke released her, and took a few steps backward. He studied her appearance with a critical look. "It wasn't what you said— it was who ya said it in front of."

DeeDee scowled. "Who I—" She cocked her head to one side and eyed him curiously. "Besides the twins, there was only Rebecca, Ruth Alice, and the minister."

Zeke gestured with a nod. "And just look at the way yer dressed. What's that all about?"

Frowning, DeeDee glanced down at her clothes. *Not you, too, Uncle Zeke.* Why should what she was wearing make a difference to him? It never had before. As a matter of fact, he had always seemed to enjoy her rebellious antics.

She looked back at her uncle and studied the way his blue and black checked flannel shirt was buttoned tightly over his generous size, all the way up to his throat. "Maybe impressin' that minister and Miss Lemon-mouth got you dressin' fer supper like some eastern dandy, but I—"

"We ain't talkin' about me," he announced in an irritated voice. Then, with obvious resignation, the heavyset man arched one very white, bushy brow and glowered at her. "And why're ya talkin' like that?"

"Like what?" DeeDee tried to sound as if she did not know what he meant. She was working very hard to make her frontier dialect sound natural.

Setting his hands on his hips again, he shook his head. "Ya know, when Aaron wrote me about yer growin' willfulness, I thought he was just—well, bein' Aaron." He hesitated a moment. "He never has seemed to warm up to ya all that much."

Warm up to her? DeeDee frowned. And what was *that* supposed to mean? The way Uncle Zeke spoke about her father's feelings toward her, one might think she had been trussed up and left on the Gallaghers' doorstep like some kind of orphan or something.

DeeDee shrugged off the thought with a silent snort. Of course, that could not be possible. Did she not possess the same large, saucer-shaped blue eyes of both her mother and Uncle Zeke? And when she was a child, had she not even developed the inherent laziness of one eye that was known to be a family trait?

Zeke sighed. "If only Aaron and Hedie May could see ya now."

"Look, Uncle Zeke, I'm just doin' what you've always told me to do."

He shook his head. "I never told ya to do nothin' like this." He gestured toward her garments again.

"Ya always told me to—ta be myself."

"Yerself?" His already large eyes widened to their fullest. "Hell, girl, this ain't you." He waved an accusing hand toward her. "This's some kinda flashy, unchecked, pretense of one of them women in them dime novels ya been readin'. This ain't you. You've always dressed . . . well—"

"Like all the other proper little namby-pamby girls in Dallas. Hmph!" DeeDee bristled.

"No!" Uncle Zeke lashed out at her, then just as quickly softened. "Like a lady."

"At least I'm bein' who I want to be." DeeDee knew all about some incident that had happened here in Harmony a while back with her uncle and the sheriff. She knew how he had helped the lawman catch some outlaw. And she had further discovered from his letters to her parents how in aiding the sheriff, Uncle Zeke had come to realize that even though he did not miss being on the run, he *did* miss the adventure of his scandalously wild youth when he, himself, had been a gunman.

He frowned. "What's that suppose to mean?"

She arched a brow. "Nothin'."

He studied her a moment.

Uncomfortable beneath his perusal, DeeDee shifted her feet slightly apart. She could not read the strange yet affectionate look in his eyes. What turmoil haunted the man?

Zeke seemed to relax a bit, then moved closer and ran an affectionate caress up her arms to her shoulders. "Why, DeeDee girl? Why're ya wantin' to be this way?" He tipped up her chin with a finger, his twinkling blue gaze boring into hers. "That's why I wrote Aaron and had him send ya out here to spend the summer with me."

Puzzled, DeeDee frowned. Her uncle was not making any sense. "I don't understand. What's why you had me come out?"

Sighing, Zeke dropped his hold on her and moved to the window. He remained silent for a drawn-out moment.

DeeDee's curiosity got the better of her. Crossing the room, she halted beside him and touched his elbow.

He glanced down at her. "I was goin' to wait a while before I told ya. I wanted ya to get to know him better." He shrugged. "And wind up likin' him on yer own."

"What do you mean?" DeeDee grimaced. "Told me what?"

"About the pastor."

"Reverend Wylie?" She shrugged. "You still think he was upset by what I said?" She chuckled softly. "Believe me, Uncle Zeke, it wasn't any big deal. Reverend Wylie thought I was funny. He almost laughed out loud. I know. I was watchin' him."

Startled by her own admission, DeeDee turned toward the glass panes and studied the empty street with overzealous enthusiasm. She had not planned on revealing the considerable time she had spent at the supper table carefully contemplating the young minister.

"Watchin' him, were ya?" Resting one arm across his girth, Zeke set the other elbow atop his hand, then rubbed his whiskered chin. "So, ya *were* interested in the pastor?"

DeeDee whirled back to face her uncle. "What's that s'pposed ta mean?"

In the lamplight his teeth flashed in a grin. "Nothin'. Nothin' at all." He waved a hand, then moved to the opposite side of the room and retrieved a broom and dustpan from a corner.

"I don't think I like the way you said *nothin'*."

Holding to silence, Zeke stooped over and swept up the broken jar pieces. Once he had collected the other shattered glass from the countertop, he dumped them into a small wastecan in the same corner where he had found the cleaning tools.

DeeDee folded her arms across her middle and squinted. "What's goin' on here, Uncle Zeke?"

"I'm cleanin' up the mess ya made," he stated dryly as he replaced the broom and dustpan.

Arching her brows, DeeDee looked past the man, studying the play of his shadow on the wall. What was he up to? He suddenly appeared to be only too happy to veer away from his explanation. She could not let him get away with that. "If that's true, then why did you say it wasn't *what* I said, but *who* I said it in front of? And what's all this stuff about liking someone?" She lifted her chin a little higher. "I can only assume you mean the reverend."

"Mmm-hmm." Moving to a wall cabinet, Zeke took a bottle from the shelf. He removed the stopper, sprinkled a few drops into his palm, then replaced the top and reset the container on the ledge. Patting the aromatic liquid onto his face, he turned toward her.

"What's going on, Uncle Zeke?" She was getting tired of asking this question.

"How's yer singin', DeeDee, girl?"

"What?"

"Yer singin'." Zeke wiped his hands on his shirt, then sent a huge smile her way. "Ya do sing, don't ya?"

DeeDee pulled a frown as if she had just swallowed a mouthful of vinegar. "Only when no one's around."

"Good—good; can't let Ruth Alice have all the fun." Suddenly looking anxious about something, Zeke moved within an arm's reach of her, then grasped her hand. "C'mon, then." He pulled her toward the door.

Bewildered, DeeDee could only follow like some puppy on a rope. Eventually he would have to tell her what he was doing—and why—would he not?

Once they stepped outside, Zeke led her down the middle of the dirt street toward the church, centered at one end of town.

From within the white clapboard building, light shone through the colorful stained-glass windows. Voices rose in harmony, growing more and more clear, sounding softly melodious above the competent accompaniment of a full-toned organ. Every human timbre added to the next, like the taste of fresh biscuits oozing melted butter and drizzling with honey.

Still in tow, DeeDee looked at her uncle. "We're going to church?"

The man nodded. "I thought you'd like to meet some more of the townsfolk. Some closer to yer own age."

"Now?" First, he berated her for her indecent comments at supper. Then, he chastised her for her clothing and dialect. He bewildered her with talk about Reverend Wylie, and someone Uncle Zeke wanted her to like . . . and now he was hauling her off to church?

The gentle sound of the river's flowing current called to her above the singing. The water—maybe it was poisoned with some strange elixir that made a person insane. That might explain Uncle Zeke's odd behavior.

Her imagination took control of her thinking. Maybe long ago some medicine man of some unknown Indian tribe had his sweetheart stolen away from him by her family.

Half-running, half-yanked along beside her uncle, DeeDee's heart beat faster, though whether it was from her movements or from her romantic notions, she did not know, and cared even less.

Maybe this Indian was so lovelorn without his lady that he became enraged with the woman's family and set about destroying them as they had done to him. Maybe he concocted an extract from some strange plant, poured it into the river, and—

"DeeDee?" Zeke snapped his fingers in front of her eyes.

"Hmm?" She blinked.

The singing had stopped and had been replaced by a rustle of murmurs.

Glancing around at her surroundings, she was startled to discover she was already inside the church.

The faces of strangers moved into focus.

"DeeDee, girl, this is Ed Winchester, our choir director. He and his uncle, Fred Winchester, own the Double B Ranch outside of town."

Confused, DeeDee slipped her gaze over to the slender man.

Zeke leaned nearer. "Wait till ya hear him talk." He winked and grinned. "He's from England."

A gray stare met hers. Crinkles at the corners of the man's eyes bespoke mirth and weather more than age. And though it was only too obvious that he took in her appearance with amusement, the man dipped his head respectfully. "It's a pleasure, Miss—um—Delilah."

Inwardly she groaned. "Why does everyone have a problem with my name?"

"Dee . . . Dee," Zeke warned in a low voice.

She smiled sweetly, then accepted the choir director's proferred hand with a hard shake. "There's no Miss—no um—just DeeDee, okay?"

"Why, of course, Miss—um—I mean—" His face flushing crimson against a frame of equally dark red hair, the man turned to his ensemble. "Everyone."

Instant silence reigned. All eyes in the group looked her way.

"In case you have not yet been introduced, this is DeeDee Gallagher." He moved back to face her. "She joins us for the summer. From?" He looked at Zeke.

"Dallas, Pennsylvania," her uncle announced pridefully. Slipping an arm around her shoulders, he teetered back and forth from his toes to his heels. "Her father's a preacher, ya know, so DeeDee here's knowledgeable in church stuff."

DeeDee felt the corners of her mouth tremble slightly as she took in the expressions of the choir members as they studied her outfit, but she was not about to allow them to defeat her smile. She would not be intimidated by these people.

"Your uncle tells me you have an interest in joining our little singing group?" Ed Winchester asked.

Funny, she had not noticed how stuffy his British accent truly was until now. Stuffy, yes, but it did bring a pleasant tone to her ear. "Actually, I'm not sure this's such a good idea."

"Why not?" Ed asked. "Weren't you in your father's church choir?"

She shook her head.

"Well, then, DeeDee, girl, how d'ya know it's not a good idea, if you've never tried it before?" her uncle rushed in, pushing her gently toward the small group. "Ed, where d'ya want her to stand?"

"Anywhere is fine, until I've heard the range and quality of her voice."

"Good—good," Zeke said, thrusting DeeDee in between Ruth Alice and Zan Winchester, Ed's wife. "You all can exchange yer 'how do's' later." He then immediately lunged back toward the rows of benches.

"All right, people," Ed said with an uplift of his hands. "Let's take it from the top."

"Amazing Grace, how sweet the sound . . ."

DeeDee did her best to stay in tune with her fellow vocalists. Sadly, though, the once-sweet warble of the choir echoed against the inner walls of the church with the sound of a caged vulture amongst songbirds.

DeeDee struggled to reach each pitch with great effort. Funny, always before whenever she had been alone and caught up in song, she had managed the various intonations very well, and had even thought she sounded quite grand.

Zeke sat on the edge of one of the middlemost pews, and smiled tolerantly, if not a bit too animatedly.

Three songs later, following along with the hymnal, DeeDee herself had to wince a time or two along with the rest of the choir as she continually tweaked a note. Why, oh, why had she not taken the time to practice her singing as her mother had asked?

At last Ed Winchester clapped his hands. "Let's take a break, shall we?" he said when the room had once again fallen into blissful silence. "Have some coffee . . . rest your voices a few minutes."

The latter he directed straight to DeeDee.

"So, um, DeeDee?" Ruth Alice cleared her throat.

*Why do they keep saying that? I wonder what kind of name they think* um *is?* DeeDee sighed indignantly, then she and Ruth Alice moved toward the refreshment table.

"You're only here for the summer?" The blond poured herself a cup of coffee.

"So far." From the corner of her eye, DeeDee watched as Ed Winchester spoke quietly to her uncle. She poured herself a cool drink and took a sip.

"And you're a preacher's daughter?"

"'Fraid so." She glanced back at the young woman's troubled expression. Studying Ruth Alice's features, DeeDee guessed the pretty blonde's age to be near her own—maybe three or four years older at most. "Why?"

"Oh, no reason." Softly shaped brows knitted, Ruth Alice pulled her bottom lip between her teeth. "Somehow, I wasn't expecting you to be quite so attractive."

DeeDee felt her cheeks warm. What a strange comment for the woman to make. "Expecting? Did my uncle tell you about me?"

Ruth Alice shook her head. Two ringlets dangling from her pile of blond curls brushed one shoulder with her movements. "Miss Minnie did."

DeeDee's eyes widened. She chuckled lightly. "But she's never seen me before tonight. What could she've known about how I look?"

Sucking in a deep breath, Ruth Alice spread her

lips into a thin smile and shrugged. "Apparently, not enough."

"DeeDee?"

Turning to the sound of her name, DeeDee looked at her uncle.

He motioned for her to join him and Ed Winchester.

"DeeDee, girl." Once she had converged on the two men, Zeke encircled her shoulders with a weighty arm. "Ed, here, says you're havin' a little trouble pullin' yer voice in with the others."

"It must be that you're tired from traveling," Ed Winchester interjected. "Zeke should not have made you join us tonight."

The way the Englishman shot a look at her uncle made DeeDee realize just how much *he* wished Uncle Zeke had not brought her, either.

"Maybe until you can accustom yourself to our way of singing, you should just mouth the words— just for a while—so you don't strain yourself." Ed Winchester peered at her with a hope-filled smile. "You understand, don't you?"

DeeDee understood only too well. The man hated her voice. She felt a twinge of irritation, but agreed with a nod and a shrug. That was okay by her. She had ears. She knew how badly she had made the group sound. And she had no desire to embarrass herself any further—especially in light of her introduction to the town this afternoon. After tonight she would simply make up an excuse for not joining the choir anymore.

"Wonderful." Ed's posture visibly relaxed and a

true expression of joy filled his features. "Well, now that that's settled. . . ." Returning to his place, he directed everyone to finish their refreshments and retake their positions in line.

Zeke pecked DeeDee's cheek. "That's my DeeDee, girl."

She shot him a sarcastic, I'll-get-even-with-you-for-this squint, then made her way back to the group. Why was it so important to her uncle for her to be in this choir anyhow? Ed Winchester had been polite enough, but he *had* insulted her singing capabilities.

Why had Uncle Zeke not whisked her out of the church? Surely he had heard how badly she sang. Was the man tone deaf? Did he not realize that she was definitely not wanted?

"Take your places, everyone." Ed raised his hands again.

DeeDee reluctantly rejoined the choir. Then realized her uncle had slipped quietly outside. She stiffened.

*Oh, no, you don't.* "I'll be right back," she called over her shoulder, then dashed toward the door. If she had to endure this humiliation, so did Uncle Zeke. It was only fair.

Still holding on to her nearly full glass, she gripped the container as if it were a weapon of great magnitude. Spotting her uncle hurrying down the street, she raced down the wood steps and called to him. "Uncle Zeke, where're you going?"

He looked back, but kept up a steady pace in the opposite direction. "I've got some visitin' to do over at The Last Resort."

DeeDee cut a glance toward the building emitting a rowdy mixture of laughter and piano music that clashed with the somber song of praise that had began inside the church again. "A saloon? My first night in town and you dump me at the church, then go to a saloon?" she railed, keeping her voice pitched as low as her temper would allow. Pinpricks of anger jabbed at her stomach.

"I knew you'd want to meet and be with people yer own age, DeeDee, girl." He motioned her back to the church. "Just go on in and have yerself a good time. Ya can go on back to the boardin' house with Ruth Alice when yer done." He wheeled around and bore down on his destination.

"Don't you do this to me, Uncle Zeke!"

But he just kept walking—no—running, toward the saloon.

"Uncle Zeke!" she half screeched.

He halted just short of the swinging doors of the barroom, then waved. "Don't fret about me, DeeDee, girl. I'll be fine." That said, the coward darted inside the noisy interior.

"Ooo!" DeeDee raged with a sound stomp of her foot. Who did her uncle think he was fooling? He must have forgotten about her arrival today, and had made some kind of seedy plans to meet up with one of his floozy women-friends.

In a huff, she snorted loudly. Hadn't her parents discussed his many illicit trysts on numerous occasions? Though she was certain her mother and father never knew she had overheard them talking about him, DeeDee had even learned of a secret love affair between her uncle and some Texas woman. But that was supposed to have been back in his notorious gun-toting days, when he was much younger. He was thought to have become more settled down now.

"Damnation!" Apparently, that was not how it was at all. And DeeDee was not about to let him get away with this. With a defiant glare she whirled back toward the church. But instead, she slammed into a solid wall of a man's chest.

Two arms caught her prisoner.

With the impact, she clutched the man around his waist to keep her balance. The glass plunged from her grasp, followed by the discernable sound of liquid shooting upward like a small geyser.

Stunned, DeeDee glanced up at her captor.

Reverend Wylie's soft brown, though somewhat abashed, stare held her immobile. He tensed, then groaned.

DeeDee heard the light patter of water dripping to the ground. Fearfully, she leaned around the man and peered down his back.

As if to taunt her, droplets of water reflected the meager evening light as they trickled down his pants to a small puddle on the ground.

She cringed. With a defeated moan, she slumped her forehead against the minister's arm and squeezed her eyes closed. *No, Lord, please.* But praying did not vanquish her offense. And even though it had truly been accidental and purely innocent, it appeared that she had managed to baptize him . . . for the third time in one day.

# ♥ ♥ Chapter 4

STANDING OUTSIDE THE church at the foot of the steps, DeeDee felt Joshua Wylie's fingers press into her sides ever so slightly. Wary of the anger she would have to encounter from him, she gripped his coat sleeves and slowly raised her head. Immediately she opened her mouth to plead for forgiveness, but seeing an unfamiliar light spark in the depths of his eyes, she held to silence.

His soft brown gaze stroked the contours of her face with a look of inexhaustible patience and remarkable understanding.

As if to taunt her alone, growing clouds danced back and forth across the full face of the moon, causing DeeDee to have to strain her vision to see him. She peered deeper.

He wore his hair a little bit longer than any other minister she had ever known. And she now found herself marveling at the way it curled behind his ears. It teased her with a sudden desire to comb her fingers through its near-shoulder length.

With strong angular planes and hollows, his face bespoke an intriguing moodiness and spiritual depth. And somewhere behind his mask of reverence, she thought she saw the distinct flicker of both heaven and hell warring within his soul . . . waiting, wanting, struggling to be released.

The clergyman arched a brow. "Well, I must say, Miss Delilah—"

DeeDee pulled away from him. "Hold it a minute."

Obviously startled, the man paused.

"Could you just please call me DeeDee? Geez." With a resentful sigh, she shook her head and turned away from him. Then, folding her arms across her middle, she stalked toward the river. All the while she muttered peevishly to herself, "I don't understand why *everybody* has such a tough time with my name."

Forgetting about the minister, she kicked at a rock on her path. "It's not that hard to say. Dee . . . Dee! Two easy words—not even words, really— only sounds. It's just one Dee, and another Dee. How much easier could a name be?" She drew back for another attack on the stone she was following.

From out of nowhere a foot appeared, punting her prey out of her reach. "None, I guess."

Startled, DeeDee flinched. She glanced up at the
minister. She had become so quickly engrossed in
her own self-imposed pity and temper that the
man's presence had almost slipped her mind. She
slowed her step, staring after him as he passed her
by and continued to kick the rock toward the river.
"You guess?" she hurried up beside him. "When're
you going to know for sure?"

"Know what?" Glancing at her, he missed the
stone.

DeeDee did not. She toe-jabbed it a few yards
ahead of him. "You said, none, you guessed." She
shrugged, keeping her focus on the skittering rock.
"So, I just want to know when you were going to
*know*."

His frown suggested he had no idea as to what
she was talking about.

Geez. Had he forgotten already? "My name—we
were talking about my name. You know . . . how
easy it is to say?"

"*We* were? Oh, yes, of course." He took his aim
on the stone, then shot it down the path another
few yards.

"Okay, *I* was." She fastened her attention on the
granite target. Where had it gone?

The clouds were growing thicker, making it
harder to see. The breeze picked up. Moonbeams
poked through the overhead haze.

There it was. She hurried toward it. "Why does
everyone here act like they're going to choke if
they call me DeeDee? Nobody back home ever
seemed to have a problem with it."

"I'm sorry. I just assumed I should use your Christian name over your nickname."

"Oh, and does—don't De-li-lah just drip outta ever'body's mouth like warmed-up honey?" She wagged her head churlishly.

Reverend Wylie halted. "Why do you do that?"

On impulse DeeDee followed suit. "Do what?"

"Talk like that."

DeeDee's mouth went dry. Had she floundered in her frontier dialect that badly? She thought she was doing rather well. She wet her lips.

Instantly his gaze dropped to her movement.

A strange tickle fluttered against her heart. "I—uh—really cain't see what you mean," she stammered.

"See, you're doing it again." He smiled, a wicked light glimmering in his eyes. "That funny speech you keep using—it's not natural, yet you keep using it. Why?"

DeeDee steeled herself against his observation. "What makes ya think it ain't natch'ral?"

He snorted a chuckle. "Because you frequently forget about using it. Like a little while ago, when you were grumbling about my calling you Delilah." He tipped his head suggestively. "You spoke quite properly then."

DeeDee waged war with her brain for some kind of flip answer. How would a dime novel heroine meet this challenge? No help came to her. Damnation. She glanced back toward town.

In the distance, choir voices softly ebbed and flowed in and around the buildings.

She flashed him a devil's smirk. "I prob'ly do it for the same reason you let Maisie and Minnie flaunt Rebecca and Ruth Alice in your face."

Reverend Wylie flinched.

At that moment, a light pattering of raindrops fell from the sky.

"What does that have to do with what we're talking—"

"When both Miss Maisie and Miss Minnie were telling you how to spend your evening, you just let them pull you along like a puppet. But did you stand up for your thoughts? Oh, no, that might be too forward."

Reverend Wylie simply stared at her.

Why did he not answer? She could see by his strained expression that he was at least a little angry.

Finally he did just that. "I really don't think you know me well enough to make such personal judgments."

She snorted. "I don't have to have known you that long. I've known too many others like you. A couple of hours is plenty of time to spot your kind. Believe me, I know. My father's just like you. If he slips and shows the true Reverend Aaron Gallagher, and does or says something that he wholeheartedly means . . ."

She leaned toward him, pumping more than an ample amount of sarcasm in her voice. "And you know he means it, then he turns around and apologizes. But, of course, he doesn't really mean that. It's just a way of covering up for his being like everybody else, Reverend Wylie—not saintly like he'd have you believe—just human."

"It's Joshua."

"What?" The rain pelted atop her head and shoulders, adding distraction to her confusion.

He smiled again with that disarmingly, understanding smile of his. "I said my name's Joshua."

DeeDee scrunched up her face with disbelief. She had just insulted him and he was asking her to call him Joshua? "My God, you *are* alike. Just change the subject, that'll fix it, huh?" She leaned her head back and let the rain pepper her face. How had she gotten into this argument? *Why* had she gotten into this argument?

As if in answer, the heavens thundered a long, deep-pitched rumble above her.

When she had left home, she had promised herself that she was never going to let herself get suckered into another dispute like this again. Now here she was sparring with someone little more than a stranger, just like she always had with her father.

A sudden rush of embarrassment washed over her with the warm droplets showering her. She had let this man see too much of her inner self, too soon. Straightening, she peered at the minister. What must he think of her, going off on that childlike tangent the way she had? He had no way of knowing how his actions would affect her. He did not know what her home life with her father had been like. And why had she attacked him with all this—especially when she did not even know him?

But most importantly, why did she care what he really thought about Ruth Alice and Rebecca and their respective benefactresses?

Looking into his rain-moistened expression of dismay, she bit back a groan. Now, even if she wanted to, she would probably never get to know him. She had embarrassed herself so badly, she could no longer face him. She glanced around for an escape.

He must have seen the look. He reached for her hand. "DeeDee—"

She did not wait—did not listen further. How could she hope to explain the reasons behind her outburst? She could not handle this right now. It was too overwhelming—even for her. She had to get away from him.

The sound of the turning mill wheel echoed in the distance.

She darted toward it. But in the darkness of the spring shower, she could not see it clearly. She could only find her way by the constant churning of water spinning the wheel.

"DeeDee?" the minister called out. "Come back. Where are you going?"

It was too far back to the boardinghouse. She would be soaked by the time she returned if she tried in all this rain. She kept charging toward the mill. There, she could get out of the rain and distance herself from him—and all she'd revealed about herself.

If he could not find her, he would go back to the boardinghouse.

She would wait until the rain let up, then she would sneak in later. And maybe, just maybe, by morning she would be able to think of a way to cover up this whole mess. Reaching the huge door to the mill, she tugged, but it appeared stuck.

The minister's voice grew closer.

Geez! Now what? He would find her if she did not leave. She looked out through the rain. She could just see the town's lights through the downpour. Unable to get inside the mill, she now had no other choice but to try and slip past the clergyman and get back to the boardinghouse.

She thought of her heroine, and how in the novel the woman had easily eluded Deadwood Sam's advances.

Reverend Wylie called to her again.

She pulled her bottom lip between her teeth. Was she as clever? Could she get away without him finding her? "C'mon, Sue. Help me outta this." Taking a deep breath, she crouched low and dashed back toward town.

Managing safely through the thicket of trees, she maneuvered her way around the buildings until she found herself standing in front of Maisie and Minnie's lodgings. She peeked inside one of the windows.

In the front parlor a small flame flickered low in a single lamp, but no one was in sight.

On reflex, she glanced around the town. Except for the bawdy laughter and music still coming from the two saloons, all remained quiet. What time was it? She judged it to be about eight, maybe nine.

Relief washed over her. Of course no one was up. As late as it was, everyone in the house must have already gone to bed by now.

She gripped the doorknob.

Barely audible, she heard the minister call her name from somewhere far off.

Sue's last words in the story came back to DeeDee. *"Obliged fer the frolic, boys! See ya in hell if not before!"*

Choosing an appropriate paraphrase, DeeDee grinned. Then, dripping wet, she saluted the minister's efforts at finding her with a smart snap of her wrist. "Obliged fer the frolic, Joshie! See ya in the mornin' . . ." She pushed open the door, then shot a final look toward the river. "But definitely not a moment before."

# ♥♥ Chapter 5

"'LYING LIPS ARE abomination to the Lord: but they that deal truly are his delight!'" In a small meadow a little more than a half mile outside of Harmony, Joshua Wylie clenched his right fist and punched the air for emphasis. He lifted the open Bible in his left palm as if to show the natural setting the page from which he read.

"This, Proverbs twelve twenty-two, is one of the first verses parents preach to their children. Yet even so, these same teachers more often than not cast out these God-given words from their hearts, choosing instead deceit as their tool when confronted with an uncomfortable situation."

He snapped the Good Book closed, clasping it to his chest in a fearsome grip. The air whispered beneath his unbuttoned jacket, but gave him little relief against the day's brooding warmth. He dug his bare toes into the cool sod, leaned forward, and squinted at a yellow cluster of newly blossomed sunflowers bobbing in the late-morning breeze. "Let me tell you a quick story from back in the early days of a political movement in Europe when Protestants were trying to break free from Catholic rule.

"Now, it happened one day after a great revolt that a visiting hawker was stopped by a small band of men on the outskirts of a village. The man knew of the strife that was going on in the land, but he wanted no part of it. So he told the fierce-looking strangers that he wished only to rest a short time, and perhaps sell some of his wares if they would only let him have safe passage."

Joshua smiled wryly and rubbed his chin, acting out the scene as he envisioned it in his mind. "'Proclaim your faith, man, so that we may see you as friend or foe,' came the voice of the formidable-looking leader."

Joshua belted out the words most dramatically. "Afraid, the man did not know what to say. If he proclaimed himself a Protestant and they were Catholic, he would be killed instantly. And he could expect the same if he were to profess the opposite, and they were the reverse." Joshua's smile broadened. "So being the wayfarer of many foreign lands, the traveler chose to tell the men that he was of the Jewish faith, and no more than a lowly peddler from the faraway land of Jerusalem."

Joshua stretched out his arm and pointed a finger at his audience of sunflowers. "So what has this to do with lies, you're asking yourselves?" He nodded knowingly, then hunched down as if he were an actor on a stage, reciting his lines. "The guards to the village weren't Protestants or Catholics. They were marauding bandits from another faraway land called Egypt. And once the poor man told his lie, they drew their weapons and smiled wickedly, hailing in a loud voice, 'Allah be praised.'"

He lowered his hands behind him and kept a firm hold on his Bible. Slowly he paced in front of the blossoms for a weighty moment. "You see my point? A lie, even for what one might truly believe to be for a *good* reason, usually gets you into greater trouble." He paused again, then cocked his head toward the flowery faces. "If the peddler had only told the truth, he would've at least had an equal chance of remaining alive, wouldn't you agree?"

At that moment a meadowlark sent up a tuneful whistle.

"'Amen' is right, Brother!" He smiled in the direction of the singing bird. "And so I say to you, good Christians of Harmony, be they for good or for evil, do not allow the devil to tempt you to use even the smallest of lies to replace truth. For, as in Proverbs twelve nineteen: 'The lip of truth shall be established for ever but a lying tongue is but for a moment.' More's the pity that this lesson was learned too late by the peddler."

Still clutching the Bible behind him, Joshua turned to fully face his imaginary parishioners.

He could almost visualize the solemn, chastised expressions of every man, woman, and child as they accepted the full meaning of his sermon. He reveled in the gratifying sensation.

If only he could truly fulfill his duties as a man of God in the church, like he had out here. If only he could deliver the Scripture so that all would actually pay attention, understand, and put His word into practice in their lives. He released a discontented sigh. If only he could preach as he had just done, maybe they would.

But, of course, anything short of fire and brimstone was not proper, as Reverend Harkington always tried to tell him. It was what people expected from their minister.

A flurry of titters intruded on his thoughts.

Startled, he snapped his attention in the direction of the sound.

The laughter rose again, this time a little louder.

He blinked against the glare impairing his vision.

A few yards to his left something stirred the tall grasses at the edge of the meadow.

"Who's there?" he called out.

"Uh-oh! He's seen us. Get goin' now," someone whispered.

Both irritated and embarrassed that he had been watched, Joshua strode toward the voice. "Show yourself!" he demanded.

As if the form had materialized upon his command, a familiar figure rose at the edge of the meadow. Garbed in a doeskin jacket and a black pair of men's britches, the woman towered over the pale stems of millet and foxtail.

"Miss—" He squinted against the full rays of the noon sun. "DeeDee? Is that you?" He smiled. Dressed like that, who else could it be? He had been trying to get a chance to talk with her privately since the incident in the rain, but, with the exception of meals, she had been avoiding any proximity with him for the last three days.

"Uh—yes, Reverend Wylie." She glanced at his chest. "It's me."

He stopped, midstride. His face flamed hot. His coat! He had forgotten about it being open.

Lowering her head, DeeDee smiled, though she kept her gaze trained on him.

"I thought I was alone out here," he said, buttoning the frock. "Who else is with you?"

Palms up, DeeDee waved her hands at the ground.

Younger faces shot up through the meadow turf.

Joshua groaned.

"I'm keeping an eye on the Lind and Tolliver children while their mothers are visiting Miss Minnie. We were just playing. We didn't know you were out here practicing your, uh—" She glanced nervously at the beaming expressions around her. "We didn't mean to disturb you."

"Y-you sure looked fu-fu-funny, Re-re-reverend Wylie," the little girl standing next to DeeDee stuttered with a giggle.

"Lizzy Tolliver?"

The little girl nodded, blond curls bobbing.

The other children laughed.

With a light swat DeeDee instantly scooted her in the direction of town. "I'm sorry for—uh—" She shooed the rest of the mischievous sprites in much the same way. "I'm just sorry. We'll be on our way now. Mrs. Tolliver and Mrs. Lind are probably wondering where we are."

"Wait!" He raised a hand. "I'd like to talk to you."

But DeeDee had already turned away. "Sorry, Reverend," she hollered with a backward wave. "Gotta git these kids back to their maws."

Joshua started after her, but something jabbed the bottom of his foot. "Ouch!" His shoes. He had forgotten about them, too. Wheeling around, he hurried back to where he had left them. He slipped them onto his feet, then snatched up his socks and stuffed them into his pockets.

He could not let DeeDee get away from him again. Not while he might finally have a chance to talk to her about their confrontation the other night. Bible in hand, he trotted after her. And if he hurried, he might be able to catch up to her before she and the children got back to town.

Nearing the gristmill, he heard childlike laughter and the echo of water splashing. Good. They had stopped for a swim. Now was his chance. He moved closer.

The millwheel groaned with a churning roar against the backdrop of happy play.

"You children don't go near that thing while it's turning." DeeDee's voice pitched even louder.

Coming upon the first tree in sight of the river, Joshua halted. He searched the area for the woman.

Several of the children who had been with DeeDee in the meadow were playing in the river. Billy Taylor and some of the older boys were also taking a swim. But where was DeeDee? Narrowing his eyes, he followed the bank toward the sound of her voice.

DeeDee sat with Lizzy and Joey Tolliver near the edge of the water.

"I wanna go swimmin'!" Joey said with a pouty frown.

"Not now," DeeDee instructed. She reached for him.

Joey jerked away, then jumped to his feet. He folded his arms tightly over his pooched-out little belly.

"Come on, Joey. It's almost lunchtime." DeeDee tried to console the little boy. "The men'll be stopping to eat soon. Then I'll take you swimming, okay?"

"Why do they get to go into the water and I can't?" He gestured toward the older children splashing in the water.

"'Cause they're all bigger than you."

"But I'm big enough." The way Joey stretched up to his full height, one might have guessed him to be *at least* a half year older than his true age of seven.

DeeDee shook her head. "Not *that* big." She pointed to the paddlewheel. "See how huge *it* is?"

The boy glared at the whirling circular frame.

Joshua, too, sent it a look, then glanced back at DeeDee.

She curled her legs around to her side, then pulled Lizzy up close, supporting her weight upright on one arm behind the little girl.

"It's not so big. The older boys play on it," Joey announced, then thrust out his lower lip and flashed the massive wheel a defiant glower. "I wanna go swim with the other kids."

Joshua chuckled. He knew just how the little guy felt. It did not seem like that long ago when he had wanted to join in play with all the children of the orphanage . . . but, of course, his reason for not being able to partake of their fun was a *crueler* one.

"I'm not responsible for the older boys."

"But—"

"Not while the wheel's spinnin', Joey, and that's final," DeeDee answered the youngster in a no-nonsense tone. Straightening, she picked some clover blossoms. "But you can sit at the edge of the water and put your feet in if you'd like. How's that?" Her voice was softer this time.

"It's not the same," Joey said in a sulking tone. Still, he marched over to the riverbank and plopped down. He scrunched his freckled face into a sullen look as he plunked his toes in the easy flow of the current.

Joshua turned his attention back to DeeDee. He watched her begin to weave together the tiny white puffballs she had picked.

Lizzy rose to her knees and crawled up behind DeeDee. "C-can I pl-pl-play with y-your hair?"

Apparently absorbed by her chore, DeeDee nodded.

Immediately the little girl set about untwisting the woman's tawny-russet braid. "You gots p-pretty re-re-red hair, DeeDee."

"Why, thank you, Lizzy." She gifted the girl with a winning smile. "I think you have pretty hair, too."

Lizzy beamed.

DeeDee kept a watchful eye on the remaining children frolicking in the water. "I noticed you have a little bit of a problem saying your words, Lizzy." DeeDee looked back to her creation.

"Mmm-hmm. Mamma s-s-says my gr-gr-great-gr-grandma had the s-same problem when she was a little g-g-girl." Lizzy squeezed her eyes closed the way she always did when she tried to talk.

Joshua moved up a little closer, though he made sure he kept out of sight. Maybe this would be a better way of getting to know the real Delilah Gallagher. He sat down on a little mound of earth behind a clump of bushes. He watched the comfortable way she visited with the child, and was amazed at the young woman's apparent transformation from coarse cowgirl to gentle guardian. It was the one and only time he had ever seen her appear to be completely relaxed.

"Did she ever grow out of it—your grandmother, I mean?"

If Joshua's observations were correct, Lizzy rarely talked to anyone in town. Now, with DeeDee, was the most talking he had ever heard from the six-year-old all at one time. How had the woman managed to alleviate the girl's shyness, and so quickly?

Lizzy shrugged. "I do-do-don't know. Sh-sh-she died before I wa-wa—" Clamping her jaws tight, she halted abruptly. "Born."

Lifting her gaze, DeeDee looked over her shoulder at the child. By her sympathetic expression, she appeared to feel the girl's frustration. "It's okay, Lizzy." She smiled sweetly, her considerate blue eyes turning almost silver in the sunlight. "We don't have to talk about it anymore."

"It's okay. I like t-t-talking to you, DeeDee." The youngster shrugged with a grin. "Be-be-besides, your n-n-name's easy for me to s-s-say."

DeeDee laughed—not a nervous or humiliated laugh—but a full-bodied, carefree laugh.

What a glorious sound. Joshua could not help but smile to himself as he watched them through the shrubbery. Now that he thought about it, he had never heard the woman break free with anything short of a deep-pitched guffaw when the occasion arose for laughter. He was quite certain that, too, was part of the rough exterior she wanted so desperately to project around others.

"I'm glad it's easy for *somebody*, Lizzy." DeeDee went back to weaving the flowers. "Joey doesn't seem to have the same trouble."

"Ma-ma-mama says th-th-that's cause he's a b-boy." Frowning, she shook her curly towhead. "B-b-boys don't g-g-git fl-fl-flicted with this like g-g-girls do."

DeeDee glanced up at the child with a curious expression. "Do you think this only happens to girls?"

Brushing a wayward strand of hair from her eyes, Lizzy turned down the corners of her mouth. "N-no b-b-boys ar-r-round here g-g-gots it. Just me."

"Hmm." Curling the small string of clover into a wreath, DeeDee twined the ends together. "You know . . . I brought some books from home with me. Maybe you'd like to learn how to read them. Maybe if we work together, we can get rid of your stuttering. What'd you think?"

"I ain't n-n-no good at re-re-readin'."

"I'm *not* any good at reading," DeeDee corrected. "And you're only going to become a good reader by *reading*. Still, you might be right." DeeDee kept her gaze trained on the garland.

"Hmm?" The little girl appeared puzzled.

What was DeeDee up to? On impulse, Joshua leaned nearer the bushes and pulled them a little farther apart.

"Well, some of the words are a little bigger than most people can handle. But now that I think about it," DeeDee continued with an impish smirk, "it was always the boys in my class that had the hardest time pronouncing a lot of the words in these books."

Lizzy jumped down beside the woman. "You m-m-mean these ba-ba-books are fr-from your school?" Her voice pitched with excitement.

DeeDee nodded. "Some of them, yes."

"And g-g-girls re-re-read 'em b-b-better'n b-b-boys?" The child's hope-filled gaze flitted to her brother.

DeeDee cast a look in the same direction, then back at Lizzy. Taking the small wreath of flowers, she set it on the girl's head, then beamed a radiant smile. "If they work very hard."

Perking up her posture as if she had just been crowned with a coronet of jewels, Lizzy reflected the woman's happy expression. "*I'll* wo-wo-work—" She sucked in a breath, held it a moment, then blew it out in a sigh. She formed her next words more slowly. "I'll tr-try hard, DeeDee. Can y-you help me learn to re-re-read better than Jo-Jo-Joey?"

"DeeDee! The men've stopped fer lunch," the boy bellowed. Jumping to his feet, Joey pointed to the slowing mill wheel, and peeled off his shirt. "Can I go in now?"

Ignoring the boy another moment, DeeDee crossed her eyes and made a puckish face at the girl. "Can you swim?"

Lizzy grinned. "Yep."

"As good as Joey?"

"B-b-better!"

"DeeDee?" Joey was not about to be ignored.

"Good." DeeDee peeled out of her jacket, and yanked off her knee-high moccasins and socks.

Grabbing Lizzy's hand, she jumped to her feet. "Well, then, you might as well start doing better than Joey right now. Okay by you?"

"Yippee!"

She helped the bouncing child out of her dress, leaving on Lizzy's shift. Then, as one, they ran pell-mell into the water, splashing and laughing.

In the waning sunlight that same evening after supper, DeeDee sat on the back lawn of the boardinghouse, with Lizzy, Joey, and the Lind children.

"What do you want to play?" she asked the kids.

"How 'bout Jack Straws," Joey said. "I'm good at that."

"Fine," DeeDee agreed. "Why don't you boys go over to the wood pile and get some long splinters— about twenty or so'll do."

Immediately, the youngsters did as she requested.

One by one, the women of the boardinghouse came out onto the porch—Mrs. Tolliver and Mrs. Lind included. At Minnie's and Maisie's request, their families had stayed for the evening meal.

Mr. Lind and Zeke remained in the parlor engrossed in a riveting game of checkers.

Joining her sister and the other women, Minnie brought out a huge tray laden with cups and saucers and a large china pot of coffee.

DeeDee sniffed. The aromatic fragrance was most appealing. But she had no desire to sit and chitchat with the twin matrons—especially seeing as how they were still trying to upstage one another by touting the virtues of their—as DeeDee proclaimed them—beloved little pets. And she had no need to hear any more *boring* details of how *indisputably lovely* Ruth Alice's singing voice was or how *positively wonderful* Miss Rebecca Ellen Russell was with Bible verses.

The way Miss Minnie and Miss Maisie went on about them—DeeDee cringed. It was enough to turn a body's stomach. And the twin matrons seemed especially bad about praising the younger women whenever Reverend Wylie was around. It seemed to her like some elaborate matchmaking game.

As if cued, the minister pushed open the screen door. "May I join you, ladies?"

"Of course, Reverend," Miss Minnie said with an exuberant smile. "Would you like some coffee?"

From beneath her bangs, DeeDee watched him shake his head in reply, then take a seat on the porch railing. Although she was not quite certain why, she found herself looking at him more and more. Remembering earlier when she had come across him in the meadow, and had witnessed him practicing his sermon, she smiled.

How wrong she had been about him the other night when she had accused him of being like her father. She was now completely in awe of his preaching capabilities. He had a special gift— a God-given power to capture his parishioners' attention and show them the way to incorporate the gospel into their daily lives.

Her father was *nothing* like Joshua Wylie. After his sermons most people barely remembered the topic of his Sunday oration.

"Here ya go, DeeDee," Joey announced, then plopped his bottom on the ground next to her. He thrust out a handful of straw-sized splinters of wood. "How're these?"

Examining them, DeeDee smiled. "I think they'll do quite nicely."

The other children gathered in a circle around her.

Lizzy scooted as close as she could get to DeeDee without actually sitting in her lap. "Wh-who goes first?"

DeeDee flitted another glance toward the porch.

"Put yer hands in." Joey paused. "Ain't cha gonna play now, DeeDee?"

DeeDee blinked, then looked back at the kids' questioning faces. "Sure I am." She flashed them a smile.

"Good. Put yer hands up." Joey started the eliminations by tapping the backs of each person's upheld fist. "Eeny minnie miney moe . . ."

The screen door creaked again, drawing DeeDee's attention away from the children.

"Oh, Rebecca, dear." Minnie jumped up from the cane rocker where she was sitting and ran to the brunette's side. "You should be resting if you're still not feeling well."

Lifting a handkerchief to her nose, the young woman sneezed fitfully.

" . . . if he hollers make him pay fifty dollars every day." Joey's small voice moved in and out of DeeDee's conscious thinking.

"I know, Miss Minnie," Rebecca answered. She sniffed daintily into her hanky. "But my room felt so unbearably stuffy, I just had to come out for some fresh air."

"Oh, you poor dear." Minnie patted her hand, then led the younger woman across the planked porch. "Take my seat. Would you like a cup of coffee?"

"Oh, yes. That'd—uh-choo! Excuse me. That'd be just lovely."

" . . . and you are not it!" Joey singsonged, then smacked DeeDee's hand.

Flinching, she turned back to the children. The boy's fist was the only one that still remained upheld. "Well, Joey, I guess you get to go first."

The little boy nodded with a grin, then tossed the reeds of wood onto the ground in front of him. Carefully so as not to disturb any others, he started to pick them up, one at a time.

DeeDee watched for another minute before she returned her attention to the adults.

"Well, I just don't see how she's going to be able to teach her Sunday school class tomorrow morning."

"I'll be all right in a few—" Rebecca sniffed again. "In a few days."

Maisie clucked softly. "But what about tomorrow? How will you teach the children in your condition? You know how lively those youngens are."

"Let's just wait and see how she feels in the morning before we go making decisions, Sister," Minnie said after pouring Rebecca her drink.

It was only too apparent to DeeDee that Maisie could not be happier at this turn of events. But why? Was she truly so competitive that she could actually be *pleased* by the young woman's illness? Surely not.

Then again, maybe DeeDee's suspicions *were* correct. Maybe the twins were genuinely vying to make a match with Reverend Wylie, pushing him toward their own contenders. Since she had first arrived and been introduced to the two young women, DeeDee had begun to believe this to be true. And the way the townsfolk smirked and chuckled whenever they saw the minister with one or both of the young women, it was becoming even more and more apparent.

"Why, just look at her, Minnie." Maisie's eyes flashed devilishly. "What she needs is a good rest and some of that herb tea you're so proud of. Wouldn't you agree, Reverend?"

"I'll be fine by morning," Rebecca assured everyone. Puffy and red, her usually mist-green eyes began to tear badly. Her once ivory skin appeared blotchy. "Re—uh-choo! Excuse me. Really I will."

Reverend Wylie looked quite concerned. "But if you're not feeling well, Miss Rebecca—"

"Oh, no." She sniffed again, glared at her used handkerchief, then wadded it up and shoved it in her skirt pocket. "As in Ezekiel forty-three two, 'And, behold, the glory of the God of Israel came

from the way of the east'. . . . Just you wait and
see. When that sun comes up in the morning, I'll
be fine."

DeeDee shook her head. The ol' gals were certainly reeling him in. *Poor guy, he doesn't even
know what they're up to!* Cocking her head to one
side, she frowned. *Then again, maybe he does. Lord
knows he doesn't seem to be too uneasy with all of
the attention the four of them give him.*

"L-l-look, DeeDee, Joey's got a-a-almost all of—
hey, DeeDee?" Lizzy tugged on DeeDee's sleeve.
"You ain't wa-wa-watchin'."

"*Aren't* watching," DeeDee corrected. She looked
down at the curly-topped girl. "And yes I am."

Apparently satisfied, Lizzy peered back at the
game.

Again, DeeDee was only able to pay attention to
the antics of the children for a short while before
she felt herself compelled to return vigilant eyes
to the porch.

"All the same," Maisie began again. "We need to
find someone."

"Who? There's simply no one else that can
replace Rebecca at this late time."

"True," Mrs. Lind piped in. She took a sip of her
coffee, then nodded understandingly. "Maybe we
should just keep the children home until services
tomorrow. That way we don't have to worry about
it, and Rebecca can get her rest."

"Please, don't make such a fuss on my account.
Besides, the children were so looking forward to me
telling them the story of David and—uh-uh-choo!"

Rebecca's small frame bolted forward with such force that she was almost propelled out of the rocker.

Reverend Wylie retrieved his own hanky from his pocket, then offered it to the fitful woman.

"Thank you." She sent him what appeared to be an attempt at a flirtatious flutter of her eyelashes, but only managed to be a pathetic batting of her watering eyes. She sniffed into the white fabric, then smiled. "The story of David and Goliath."

"But I can see that you're not feeling well, dear." Minnie sighed heavily. She flashed Maisie a so-you-won-the-battle, I'll-get-you-next-time look. "Maybe you should stay home, dear."

DeeDee returned her attention to the children, glancing down just in time to see Joey move two splinters while trying to retrieve another.

He groaned.

The others applauded.

"Okay for you, young man." DeeDee patted his head. "I thought you were going to get them all before I could have a turn. How many did you pick up?"

"Seventeen," he announced jubilantly.

"Hmm, I doubt I can beat that many." Gathering the sticks, she tossed them onto the ground. Then, pursing her lips, she leaned forward and began to lift away the long splinters of wood.

The kids grew quiet. Then, with each stick DeeDee successfully reclaimed, they moaned in unison.

From somewhere in the recesses of her consciousness, the minister's voice broke through her
concentration. "I think she'd be perfect. Just look at
how she gets on with the children."

"But she acts so ... so ... you know"—Mrs.
Tolliver's voice pitched low, but was still
audible—"uncivilized. I don't know if it would
be good for the children to spend so much time
with her."

"Why, Nancy Tolliver, I can't believe you said
such a thing," Mrs. Lind scolded. Mrs. Lind's
daughter Zan had been something of a tomboy
herself. "The Reverend's right. I think she'd be
wonderful. And the children do so seem to adore
her. Besides, it's only for this one time. What can
it possibly hurt?"

"Let the girl try," Maisie announced. "After all,
she _is_ a minister's daughter."

DeeDee froze in the middle of a movement. The
stick teetered on her finger. _Oh, please don't let
them be discussing who I think they are._

"Miss DeeDee?" Reverend Wylie called out.

She tried to swallow back the huge lump that
was forming in her throat, but it fought her breath
all the harder. Careful not to drop the stick, she
looked back at the minister.

He smiled, his teeth flashing white in the dimming light of day. "You've probably noticed that
Miss Rebecca isn't feeling all that well."

DeeDee cut the young woman a nervous look,
then glanced back at the man. Why was her stomach suddenly turning somersaults? She nodded.

"Well, we've all just been discussing it, and we'd like it if you'd consent to taking over her Sunday school class. It's on the story . . ."

DeeDee's eyes rounded. He was serious! One by one, she took in the expectant expressions of the minister, Rebecca, and Ruth Alice.

Mrs. Lind and Mrs. Tolliver both smiled and nodded.

"So, will you?" Reverend Wylie asked.

DeeDee tried to hold back a shiver, but it got the better of her. She swallowed. No, she just could not—would not. If she started turning into a goody-goody now, it would go against everything she was trying to be. But before she could open her mouth, the screen door banged.

"DeeDee, girl." Zeke strode out onto the porch, a big grin mocking her surprise. "Tell 'em you'll be happy to do it."

She shook her head slowly. Had he been listening all along?

Obviously hearing the conversation, the children now entered their pleas.

"C'mon, DeeDee."

"It'll be fun."

"You g-g-gonna teach us Su-su-sunday sc-sc-school?"

"Oh, boy!"

DeeDee dropped the twigs. This was not happening. It could not be. It was just like the other night, when Zeke had taken her to the church. She had not wanted to go, but he had taken her just the same. It was almost as if he, too, were in on Maisie and

Minnie's little matchmaking. Did he think he was
going to be able to use *her* as a pawn like the twins
were using Rebecca and Ruth Alice? Was that his
real reason for inviting her for a summer visit?

She blinked. *Oh, no, you don't, Uncle Zeke.
You're not goin' to manipulate me again.* Why,
oh, why, had he chosen just this moment to come
outside?

"Just look at her. She's so pleased, she don't
know what to say." Beaming like a prideful father,
Zeke reached out and shook the minister's hand.
"She'd love to do it."

"Yippee!" the children shouted. Then, clasping
hands, they began to dance around DeeDee,
singing all the while. "DeeDee's gonna teach us.
DeeDee's gonna teach us."

Unable to come up with an excusable way to
get out of the job, she winced. Then, after slicing
her uncle with a razor-sharp scowl, she suddenly
smiled. A wickedly delightful plan formed in her
mind—one that was certain to embarrass the man
into his proper place. *What I'm goin' to teach them
isn't half as much as the lesson you're goin' to learn,
Zeke Gallagher.* She spread her lips into a wider
grin and nodded. *Just you wait and see.*

# ♥ Chapter 6 ♥

IN THE LARGE storage closet of the church, Joshua leaned down to retrieve a box of hymnals from the floor. As usual, he remained as quiet as possible so as not to disturb the Sunday school classes. Closing the door behind him, he set about placing them on the pews, every yard or so. He glanced up and smiled at the one of the older boys.

Apparently allowing his mind to wander from his teacher's roll call, the young man blinked when he saw that the minister was watching him. Nothing else was needed to get the boy to return his attention back to the class. At least it seemed Joshua had some authority with the children.

Realization gripping his senses, Joshua stilled his movements. He looked around the large interior.

There was only one group participating in Sunday school. He tensed. Where were the little ones? And where was DeeDee? She *had* promised to teach them, so where was she?

The richness of her voice moved in on his hearing. He looked back at the front greeting room of the church.

Sunlight spilled inside through the partly open door.

He moved discreetly toward it, halting just behind the oak partition, and listened to her speak.

"You've all probably heard how Miss Rebecca isn't feelin' well today."

Making sure that no one saw him, Joshua moved up a little closer, peeking out through the crack separating the hinged door and the jamb. He shifted closer for a better view and squinted through the slit, but he was only able to see her profile.

Off to one side, sporting a fringed buckskin skirt that halted just below the knees, DeeDee stood on the top landing of the church, smiling down at the expectant faces of her Sunday school class. With only an occasional nod of welcome, she waited silently until everyone had quieted, then raised her hands. "Now, since Miss Rebecca can't be here, your parents have asked me to teach your Sunday school lesson today. Is that all right with all of you?"

"Do you know the story of David and Goliath, too?" one small child asked.

"Sure do."

"Well . . . I dunno . . ."

"Are ya sure ya know it?"

DeeDee grinned down at the questioning children. "Well, I tell you what. Let's just try me and see." She tapped her finger on the breeze as if it were one of their noses. "And you let me know how I do afterward, okay?"

All nodded, then started up the planked steps.

She held up her hands. "But not in there."

"Why? You afraid to be in there or somethin'?" Billy Taylor asked.

Joshua tensed. He had forgotten that the boy was going to be in her class today.

"Aren't you a bit old to be with these children?" she inquired.

Billy kicked at the dirt, then shrugged. "I got in trouble in my class last Sunday, so my ma and Reverend Wylie said since I couldn't behave with the older kids, I might oughta try bein' with the little 'uns."

Youthful titters rose around him.

"I see." DeeDee pursed her lips.

Remembering the incident with him upon her arrival, Joshua thought maybe he should override the boy's punishment for DeeDee's sake. He started to step out from behind the door but halted at the sound of the woman's footsteps.

DeeDee descended the steps, then came to stand in front of Billy. "Well, then, you're welcome here. But only so long as you know that I won't tolerate

any pranks. One chance and you're out, understand?"

The children giggled.

Billy drew his mouth into a thin line, then looked
away. "Yes'm. My ma already told me."

Joshua studied the boy's subdued posture. Billy
Taylor was not all that bad—maybe a little more
devilish than most, but that was probably due to
his inquisitive nature, and the fact that he wrote
the gossip column for the Harmony *Sentinel*. And,
too, it seemed he had to have a special need for
personal attention. Joshua smiled. He could well
relate to wanting that, himself.

"Okay, Billy, I believe you."

He offered her a half-smile, then gestured toward
the church with a nod. "So where're we goin' if we
ain't goin' inside?"

DeeDee gestured around to the side of the
building. "How about under that big cottonwood
there?"

"Outside?"

Joshua, too, was astonished. He had often
thought of holding one of his sermons outdoors,
but he did not think that would be acceptable to
the township. It was hard to imagine a woman like
Lillie Taylor sitting on the grass.

DeeDee grinned. "Why not?" She looked up at
the bright sky. "It's such a beautiful day. I'm
sure the good Lord wouldn't want us to miss
even an hour of it." Scooping Lizzy Tolliver's
hand into her own, she led the way around the
church.

Joshua's curiosity got the better of him. He found himself drawn to know how she would handle this class. After pushing the door closed, he reentered the sanctuary and began setting out the hymnals on the opposite side of the room.

Slowly, strategically, he made his way back to the closet. He opened it, then replaced the empty box on the floor. Turning around, he peered out the window only a couple of feet from the door. *What a good vantage point.*

A thought struck his consciousness. If he remained just inside the closet, he could watch DeeDee and the children and not be seen himself. He peeked around the partition at the other class.

Apparently, no one had observed his movements.

Still, it would not be right to spy on her. But his curiosity persisted. He should not have allowed himself time to question his intentions. The more he darted glances between the window and the other class, the more appealing the idea became.

With careful nonchalance, he moved to the window and lifted it, bracing it open with a wood support. Then, after one last reassuring look to see that no one in the older children's class had noticed him, he stepped back inside the closet and watched.

DeeDee's group had all seated themselves beneath the huge tree with her positioned in front of them.

With this side view Joshua could see her course of action clearly.

"So, now," she began with enthusiasm. "Let me tell you the story of David and Goliath. It begins in First Samuel, Seventeen twenty-one."

Immediately those who had Bibles flipped through the pages until they found the chapter.

Tapping a finger to her pursed lips, DeeDee slowly paced in front of the children. It appeared as if she might be a little hesitant to start.

"Well, are ya gonna tell us, DeeDee?" a little voice asked.

Lifting the length of her hair off her back, she straightened the ropes of Indian beads she wore around her neck, then tossed her mass of curls over her shoulder. She held to silence a minute more while rolling up the sleeves of her turquoise shirt to her elbows.

Joshua leaned against a stack of boxes and folded his arms across his chest. Strange, she appeared almost unsure of herself. Surely the young woman had taught a class before.

The moment grew longer.

Why did she hesitate? After another unsettling second or two, Joshua became concerned. Would he have to go to her aid? And if so, how would he explain his knowing of her dilemma?

At that instant she took a deep breath. Then, scowling, she looked off toward the rolling horizon. "See there," she said, shielding her eyes as if she were studying something in the distance.

Stretching their bodies up tall, each child strained to look in the direction she had indicated.

Joshua leaned forward a little, straining his vision toward the skyline touching the outlying hills.

"It happened long ago in a place just like that." She lowered her voice as if she were telling a secret. "Two great warring armies of Injuns."

"Injuns?" Billy piped up with a sarcastic snort. "That ain't the way I heard it."

DeeDee glared at him.

With obvious understanding that he had just had his *one chance*, he lowered his head. "Sorry."

Without further hesitation, DeeDee continued. "Now, these *Injuns,* one tribe called the Israelites, the other a vast nation of renegades called the Philistines, came to battle. Now, each side knew that they'd likely as not lose one heck of a lot of warriors if they was to act'ally fight." With each sentence DeeDee appeared to slip deeper and deeper into her storytelling role. Her speech reflected that of the rowdy, frontier character he had become accustomed to seeing her portray.

"So them there Injuns, bein' of the smart variety like they was, decided to call themselves up one champeen from each side to do their fightin' fer 'em. Whichever was to win would be the lolla-palooza for their side, an' that side would be the victor." She wheeled back to face the children. "So them there savage Philistines, ya know what they did?"

Round-eyed, most of the kids shook their heads.

Joshua grinned. She had the children completely entranced.

"Why, they got themselves a big . . . huge . . .
bull of a—" She paused effectively, then jumped
at the children with a shout. *"Giant!"*

The youngsters flinched.

Joshua almost laughed aloud, but held himself
restrained. She was really something, that one. She
was in total control of their attentions.

"Now, this here giant was called Goliath, and
he was just about the meanest, orneriest critter this
side a the Great Divide." She acted out her next
description with apparent enthusiasm. Spreading
her feet wide, she raised her hand as if she were
some huge beast. "Goliath stood nigh on to nine
an' a half foot tall." She raised her hand in obvious
indication of Goliath's height.

The children followed her movements, lifting
their gazes skyward.

"He wore a chest-plate of solid brass weighin'
over three thousand pounds with a matchin' head-
band and leggin's, too. An' his spear"—she shivered dramatically—"why, it weighed pert near *four
hundred pounds* by itself."

Some of the kids stirred nervously in their seated
positions.

Impressed with her knowledge and ability to
translate the Bible's description into simple terms,
Joshua arched a brow.

And she truly seemed to be enjoying herself. It
was the same as when she had been with the children the day before by the river. Rearing back, she
set her hands on her hips. "Needless to say, when
that ol' Goliath yelled out his challenge to them

there Israelites, there wasn't 'zactly too many takers. Matter a factly, the only one who made a move was a very small, very untrained kid—a shepherd boy—no older'n some a you."

Joshua watched the children peer at her with skeptical expressions.

"It's true!" she assured them. "And as if that weren't enough, ya know what was even more remarkable?"

They shook their heads, their eyes almost bulging with interest.

"All's this little shepherd boy armed hisself with was some rocks from a stream and a leather sling." DeeDee pretended to swing the imaginary weapon.

As one, the children sucked in an audible groan.

At that moment the door to closet swung wide.

Joshua jumped with a start.

"Oh, 'scuse me, Reverend." It was one of the boys from the older Sunday school class. "We need some—uh—whatcha lookin' at?" the kid inquired with an over-the-shoulder glance toward the window.

Joshua straightened. How was he to explain his actions?

The youth turned back to face him with a grin. "Watchin' that Delilah girl, huh?"

The hairs on the back of Joshua's neck stiffened, his muscles went taut. He did not like the sarcastic inflection in the boy's tone, nor the insinuation. "Why aren't you with your class?"

"Oh, yeah." The young man blinked. "I come for chalk."

Wheeling away from the youth, Joshua gritted his teeth. He felt as if it was the boy spying on *him* rather than him spying on DeeDee. He plundered through the boxes. Maybe if he just found what he wanted, the boy would go away without making further mention of this incident. Locating a half-full container of chalk sticks, he whirled back and shoved them at the youth. "Is this enough?" He fought to keep the urgency, not to mention irritation, from his voice.

Opening the box, the freckle-faced kid grinned. "We only need a couple."

"Take the whole thing," Joshua grated louder than he had meant. Then, sucking in a reluctant breath, he softened his tone. "You might need them." He forced a smile.

The young man nodded with a shrug. "Okay." He turned to leave.

Joshua relaxed a bit too soon.

The kid stopped and peered back with a grin. "And don't worry." He gestured toward the window. "I understand how you might feel ya need to watch that Delilah woman with them little 'uns." That said, he marched off, repositioning the door where it had been before he had intruded.

Joshua released a slow sigh. He gripped his fists at his sides. Folks' reactions to DeeDee were definitely testing his patience, not to mention his temper. Some had just made up their minds about her due to her choice of dress, her rowdy act, and the Biblical suggestion of her name. He glanced up just in time to see DeeDee lift her arm in a whirling motion.

Immediately following, she clutched her chest, groaned loudly, painfully, then stumbled a few steps and plummeted to the ground.

Joshua straightened. He had all but forgotten about her narration. He strained to hear the remainder of the tale, but it was over.

The children appeared suspended in a trance. Not one moved. Not even Billy Taylor.

All at once, DeeDee jumped to her feet and grinned.

A roar of jubilant applause signaled the children's sudden return to reality.

DeeDee bowed with dramatic flair.

A tromping of footsteps against the hardwood floor of the church grabbed Joshua's attention. From the corner of his eye he saw that the older group was leaving the sanctuary. He pulled out his pocket watch. Was the hour up so soon? He checked the time. Nine-twenty-nine. He looked out at the children and DeeDee.

All heads were yielded in silent prayer.

Joshua shook his head in envious admiration. *If only I possessed such a gift. If only I could stir the hearts and minds of my congregation as she did with these children today. . . .*

DeeDee dismissed her excited class just as the members of the church choir began to arrive.

Ruth Alice was one of the first to approach. "My, oh, my," she said, straightening her hat as if one of the blustery youngsters had knocked it askew when they dashed past her. "You certainly must have made quite an impression on them. Why, just look at the little tads." She nodded toward a couple of kids acting out the roles as they had witnessed earlier.

DeeDee smiled pridefully. What had started out as a vengeful ploy against her uncle had turned into being quite a lot of fun. She did not remember enjoying herself so much in a very long while. "Yes, I do believe they had a good time."

"Mmm." Ruth Alice lifted a brow. "But weren't they supposed to learn the story of David and Goliath today?"

DeeDee frowned at her. "You can have fun and learn at the same time."

"That's true, I suppose," the blond woman said with a shrug. "I just don't believe I've ever seen them quite so keyed up after a Bible lesson."

DeeDee combed her fingers through her hair as she walked toward the entrance of the church. "Maybe it's just because I'm somebody new. You know how feisty kids get when they have a substitute for anything?" She did not want to tell Ruth Alice that perhaps Rebecca simply had a dull way of teaching—even though, after observing the children's enthusiasm after class, that was what DeeDee believed.

Ruth Alice halted her at the foot of the steps.

"You want me to ask Miss Minnie and Miss Maisie to save you a place on their pew?"

"No—why?"

Glancing down at DeeDee's moccasins, then up at her attire, Ruth Alice swallowed. "I—uh—thought you were going home to dress for church."

Inwardly DeeDee cringed. Why did everyone make such a fuss over her clothes? And why did it matter so much what she wore? Geez. At least she *was* covered. But, even now, the way Ruth Alice was giving her the once-over, a person might think DeeDee was nearly naked. She inhaled slowly, praying for self-control, then smiled. Maybe once people got to know her, she would be more readily accepted. "I *am* dressed, Ruth Alice. I saved this outfit especially for church today."

"Oh, I see." Ruth Alice looked as if she had just bitten into a lemon and did not want anyone to know it.

One of the other members called to the young woman from the church landing.

"If you'll excuse me, DeeDee, I need to get situated in the choir."

"Of course." DeeDee nodded her approval. She was only too willing to be left on her own again. She waited a little while longer, hoping to sit with Zeke. She figured she would be safe with him. But when the church bells rang out signaling the beginning of Sunday services and Zeke had not yet arrived, DeeDee was forced to go inside unescorted.

Once she stood within the walls of the sanctuary, it did not take her long to find an empty spot toward the rear of the building. But what looks she got. And all the whispering.

DeeDee staved off a shiver. For all her strength of character and determination, after only a few minutes she wanted nothing more than to jump up and run outside.

She felt a hand on her shoulder and jumped. Glancing up, she relaxed.

Smiling, Zeke winked, then gestured for her to move over with a nod.

Joyfully DeeDee did as requested. In spite of the fact that he had backed her into a corner the previous evening, she could not be happier to see him right now.

DeeDee was looking forward to Joshua Wylie's sermon. She had been so infatuated with the powerful way he had preached in the meadow the morning before that she actually found herself anticipating the services.

After three hymns from the choir, Reverend Wylie finally moved up to the podium. Dressed in a fine black suit, his shoulder-length hair fell back from his face with only a slight part off to one side.

DeeDee swallowed convulsively. This anxious feeling of expectation was something she had not experienced in church for a very long time. And she could not ever remember having the strange fluttering sensation whorling in her stomach as it was now. Was it just apprehension—or something more? Unable to answer, she held herself in control, yet relished the disquieting rush.

After opening his Bible, Joshua leveled his gaze on the audience. *"If we say we have not sinned, we make him,* Jesus Christ, *a liar, and his word is not in us."* He searched the room as if he was looking for someone. His gaze appeared to settle on her for a long moment. "Is there ever a reason to lie?"

DeeDee held her breath. Oh, no. He would not.

As if he felt her discomfort, he looked back at the book. "According to John two twenty-one, the answer is no." He began to read the passage. *"'I have not written unto you because ye know not the truth, but because ye know it, and that no lie is of the truth.'"*

As DeeDee listened to the dry monotone of his sermon, the lump in her throat slowly diminished. Where was the fire and passion—the magic she had heard in his practice the previous day? She peered around the room and watched as most people settled into the usual unaffected expressions she had witnessed in her own father's church.

Two boys at the other end of the pew sat playing a game of scissors, rock, paper.

Some of the all-too-less-than-enthusiastic men had already started to nod off. Every now and then their spouses would nudge them awake.

She could only clearly see the rows of faces around her. But upon studying the ones that she could observe, she determined that more pairs of eyes than she could keep count were focused off into the distance.

And oh, how easy it appeared to be for some of

the young ladies and gents to let their focuses stray from the sermon to their apparent beaus only a seat or two away from them.

Her gaze moved beyond the man at the podium, to the choir. Even they appeared to be lost in their own realms of pondering. No one was paying the least bit of attention to what was being said.

Suddenly disenchanted, disappointment settled hard in DeeDee's heart. She glanced up at the minister.

"James three fourteen tells us, 'No matter what the circumstances . . . if ye have bitter envying and strife in your heart, glory not, and lie not against the truth.'"

DeeDee ground her teeth together. What had come over the man? A dead stump would show more life than the minister now displayed. Even his voice was hollow.

She suddenly felt cheated. His practice had been a ruse—a charade. Damnation! It was all so confusing. The room closed in on her.

Was the man blind? Did he not realize how ineffective his sermons were?

Her face warmed. Her temper got the better of her. Of course he did. And he did not care.

She narrowed an angry stare on Reverend Wylie. How pious he must feel, knowing *he* was the only one that understood his preaching. It was not right. The word of God should be taught so that all might come to realize His love as well as His laws.

What a child she had been to let herself be fooled

into thinking Joshua Wylie wanted to make a difference. And he spoke of lies—hmph! Rising, she
stepped around her uncle's bulk, nearly losing her
balance and falling onto his lap in her haste.

"DeeDee, girl," Zeke whispered in a worried
tone. "You all right?"

But she did not pause to give him a response. She
had to get out of there—now—before her temper
got the better of her and she screamed out the *truth*
of the clergyman's inherent injustice.

# ♥ Chapter 7

CHARGING OUT OF the church and into the sunlight, DeeDee shot a glance across the street at the bright pink boardinghouse. No. She did not want to go back to her room just now.

The warm murmur of the spring-kissed breeze whispered across her face, carrying the clean scent of the river. Yes. She needed time to be by herself, and the waterway was the ideal spot to sit and think.

"DeeDee?" Zeke ran outside after her. "What's wrong?"

But before he could even descend a single step, DeeDee had already set a hasty pace toward the river. "Not now, Uncle Zeke," she said with a backhanded wave. She had no desire to talk to anyone just yet. She was too angry, too upset.

Zeke, too, appeared just as troubled—so much so that he did not give up his pursuit. He followed her to the water's edge. Upon catching up to her, he grabbed her elbow.

She was so immersed in the whirlwind of her own emotions, she jumped, nearly losing her balance and teetering into the current.

Zeke turned her around to face him in one smooth move. "You want to tell me what's goin' on here now?" His tone demanded a response. "Why'd you tear outta there like that?"

"Please, Uncle Zeke, can't you just leave me alone for a while?"

He squinted at her, seemingly to ponder the question. "No," he answered after a couple of seconds. "I don't think I can."

With a resentful sigh, DeeDee eased out of his grasp. "Look, I'm not a child any longer. I need some—"

"Well, then if that's the case, maybe ya should stop actin' like one," he said harshly.

DeeDee blinked. Never had her uncle spoken to her in such a gruff manner.

Hands on his hips, Zeke looked up through the branches of the cottonwoods lining the riverbank and released an audible breath. After a moment of silent perusal, he leveled his gaze back to her. "C'mon." He motioned down the bank of the water. "Let's take a walk."

DeeDee rolled her eyes. "I'd really like to be by—"

"Well, that's just too bad now, ain't it, girl?" Zeke held his position. He pierced her with a look that left no mistaking he meant for her to mind him.

DeeDee swallowed. He appeared every bit as determined to talk to her now as he had been in the barbershop on the evening of her first arrival. What was she to do? She could not give into him. She *was* a grown woman. And she *was* entitled to the privacy of her own thoughts. Still, she had no desire to repeat any form of Wednesday night's events.

He dipped his head in the direction of the footpath he had just indicated, then looked at her as if to ask, ya gonna go on yer own or am I gonna carry ya?

Okay, she would go with him, but that did not mean she had to talk. Lifting her chin, DeeDee relented. With purposeful steps, she followed his lead.

"So," he said after they had been walking for a few minutes. "You goin' to tell me what that was all about back there?"

Eyes focused on the ground ahead of her, DeeDee left her answer to a shrug.

"Ya know, since ya been here I've pretty much let ya do whatever ya was a mind to."

DeeDee snorted silently. Sure he had—as long as it was what *he* wanted her to do.

"I don't think I been too demandin' in any of my requests, do you?"

Requests? She wanted to shout the word, but managed to hold her silence. She squared her shoulders and looked out at the rippling current.

"Okay, so maybe they wasn't 'zactly requests."

Her mind churned like the river. He was right about that.

"Maybe I shouldn'a made ya try out for the church choir like I did." He paused as if waiting for her to speak.

She did not.

"And maybe I shouldn'a stepped in 'bout ya teachin' the Sunday school class like I did, nei-ther—but ya gotta know I meant well." He leaned her way and looked at her with a hope-filled expression. "Ya do know that, don't ya, DeeDee, girl?"

Ignoring his plea, she breathed in deeply, her gaze trained on the landscape. She was determined to remain quiet. If *he* wanted to purge his guilt by spilling his insides to her, that was fine, but that did not mean that she was obliged to accept his apology—meager as it might be.

"DeeDee!"

She flinched. Shocked by his sudden change of tone, she felt a rush of blood to her face.

He halted. "Ya hear what I'm sayin', girl?"

She gulped back. "Yessir," she finally acknowl-edged.

"Then I'll thank ya to at least show me enough respect to answer me when I'm talkin' to ya."

Fighting to keep her bottom lip from trembling, she nodded. "Yessir, Uncle Zeke."

He studied her for a long moment, obviously trying to determine her sincerity. "Good. Now—"

With a one-eyed squint, he peered around at their surroundings.

DeeDee followed his appraisal. What was he looking for? They were a good distance away from town. She could barely see the church steeple through the treeline.

"How's 'bout we take ourselves a little sit-down over yonder?" he asked, pointing to a large drooping willow. "That okay by you?"

"Mmm-hmm." She still was not up for a full conversation. She followed him to the tree and sat beneath it, drawing her legs up beside her.

Zeke plunked himself down with a hard thump. Then, with what appeared to be great effort, he coiled himself into a cross-legged position. Snatching up a stem of grass, he peeled off the outer hull, then put the bottom end in his mouth. He seemed to be struggling to find words.

DeeDee did not offer any form of assistance. She did not know what to say and would not have said it if she had.

"Ya know," he started out, his gaze following the moving water, "I ain't your father, Aaron. Ya can talk to me if yer havin' troubles."

Turning her attention to him, DeeDee frowned. What did he mean by that? And how could he possibly know how she felt about her father? She had never told him. She had never discussed it with anyone. Not even her closest girlhood friends knew. She had always been able to put on a good act where her father was concerned.

"Ya think I don't know how it is with you and Aaron?"

"I know he wrote and told you I was becoming bothersome and insolent."

Chewing on the end of the grass, Zeke nodded. "That he did."

"That's why you asked me to come and stay with you, isn't it—to give him and mother a little peace?"

"Not completely." He glanced at her. "Now that yer older, I thought it might be a good idea for us to get to know each other a little better."

She would prefer nothing more than to get to know her uncle. She only knew bits and pieces about him, but what she had learned as a child had sounded very exciting. DeeDee studied his rough features. Except for that innate spark of light that always seemed to twinkle in his blue eyes, the man looked like he might have spent his entire lifetime riding through hell and back. She genuinely felt sorry for him. For besides the one woman that had been killed down in Texas when he was young, as far as DeeDee knew, Zeke had never been in love.

"Why don't ya tell me what's goin' on with you and the parson," he blurted out all at once.

Startled, DeeDee remained silent. How had he guessed who she was upset with?

"C'mon, DeeDee, girl." He flashed her a toothy smile. "Remember when ya was little and I was around?"

She nodded.

"Ya'd talk to me then." He shrugged. "It ain't no diff'r'nt now. Ya can still talk to me. I ain't gonna tell nobody else."

DeeDee sucked in a long drawn-out breath. He was right. She knew she could tell her uncle anything, and no one else would ever find out by his hand.

"It'll make ya feel better," he coaxed further.

She chewed on her bottom lip. What did she have to lose? "You've been to Father's sermons before."

He scowled at her, but nodded.

"Well, over the years I've come to see him for the person he truly is."

Zeke's attention shifted to the small piece of ground between them.

"I mean, he preaches God's way, then goes about his daily life another."

Zeke lifted a weighty glare onto her. "I think ya better explain that one to me. I ain't never seen anythin' but good come outta Aaron."

"Yeah." DeeDee flashed him a smirk. "That's what he wants everybody to see."

"But *you* know better, hmm?" He suddenly sounded perturbed.

"Uncle Zeke, it's true," she said defensively. "You just try doin' somethin' wrong and see if he doesn't yell at you for doin' it."

Zeke scrunched his face into a confused expression. "Is that what you two's problem was? Aaron hollered at ya a lot?" He chuckled.

DeeDee shook her head. "It's not just the yellin'." How was she to explain how she felt? She was confusing herself. She took a minute to gather her thoughts. "He can always tell you how you're supposed to live your life by God's laws and with love in your heart. But all the while he's just waitin' for a good chance to clobber you with fire and brimstone. And his sermons—"

She rolled her eyes. "It's as if he purposely chooses meaningful subjects, then preaches them so lifelessly that no one pays attention—as if he *doesn't* want anyone to pay attention. He and Reverend Wylie *are* just alike. They don't want anyone to truly live by God's ordinances." The reason for their actions suddenly came to her with crystal clarity. "Geez! That's it."

"What's it?" Zeke stared at her as if she had just swallowed a worm.

"Don't you see? If they were to make everybody else understand as they should, the ministers of the world would be out of jobs."

Zeke scowled at her, then split his face into a wide grin. He laughed out loud, long and hard.

Why? There was nothing humorous in her conclusion. If anything, it was frightening.

"Is that what ya really think?"

"That has to be it." DeeDee was equally as shocked by her deduction. It shocked her, but it *was* the only clear-cut answer.

"Oh, DeeDee, girl," he said in a patronizing tone, then shook his head.

A coil of anger snaked through her. Damn him. He was laughing at her. Her Uncle Zeke was actually laughing at her reasoning. "Stop it!" She could feel the tears forming. He had hurt her feelings. She started to jump to her feet. "Stop it!"

"No—no." He grabbed her hand and pulled her down to face him. "Wait a minute. I didn't mean to make ya upset, girl."

She would not look at him. For try as she might to hold back the tears, one spilled down her cheek in a scalding betrayal.

"Look," he said reaching over and brushing away the moisture.

She held her attention away from him.

"Look at me, girl."

Slowly DeeDee shifted her gaze to his.

"I'm sorry." He appeared sincere. "Listen," he said after a few minutes. "Maybe neither Aaron nor the parson there knows how to preach like yer talkin' 'bout. Maybe—"

"Joshua does."

Zeke's brows vaulted in a look of surprise.

"I heard him—yesterday."

"Ya did?"

She nodded. "I was playin' with the Lind and Tolliver kids. We came across him practicin' in a little meadow on the west end of town."

"Hmm. I thought that was you I heard."

DeeDee's eyes rounded. "You were out there, too?"

"Nah." He pointed in the same direction. "I was at the river fishin'. I heard ya and that noisy group of kids go tearin' down to the swimmin' spot by the mill. Didn't know who it was fer sure till I got back to the boardinghouse and saw ya with all them young'uns."

"I don't under—"

"I got up early yesterday mornin' and went out to the south fork of the water. I saw the parson come by. We exchanged how-do's, and he went on his way." Zeke shifted the grass stem to the other side of his mouth. "I knew what he was up to. I come across him doin' his practicin' like that before."

"So you know what I'm talkin' about?" DeeDee looked off to the distance. "He was *so* good, Uncle Zeke. It nearly took my breath away just listenin' to the way he spoke. He made everythin' so clear, so real." She blinked, then glanced back at the man. "Even the children were captivated."

Zeke nodded as if he understood completely.

"Then this mornin', when I heard his sermon—" She flinched. "It was just like Father's, cold, unfeeling, without hope of provoking interest. And he was just reading it."

Zeke smiled a secret smile. "And that's why you ran outta church like ya did?"

DeeDee sighed. "I was so disappointed. I had been so excited at the prospects of hearin' his sermon."

"And ya think he let ya down, hmm?"

"Oh, Uncle Zeke, he was so good yesterday—like one of my dime novels. He was so interestin'—so movin'. I've never heard any other minister preach so powerfully before."

Zeke cocked his head to one side and studied her. "Ya know he's only been here a few weeks. Maybe the parson's a little shy. Maybe he's worried how the folks'll take him if he was to preach like that. Like ya said, it is a bit diff'r'nt from normal."

"But that's just it. It's so different, it's wonderful." She felt that same fluttering in her stomach as when she had been talking to the minister himself that night by the river. "If anyone can bring these people to know God's word for what it truly is, Joshua can do it." She looked back at her uncle and smiled. "I know he can."

"Joshua, huh?" He smiled as if he had just come across some great secret. "Ya kinda like him, don't ya, girl?"

A strange quiver shot up DeeDee's spine. She had not considered the thought until now. Too late, she realized her mistake at revealing her emotions. She stiffened her spine. "I like the way he preaches—at least, the way he *can* preach when he wants to."

"Hmm." Zeke pursed his lips thoughtfully. "Well, that's a start."

She peered deeper at him. "What's a start?"

He shrugged. "Nothin'. It's just good that you've finally found somethin' to like 'bout this town. And I'm purty sure the parson likes you, too."

DeeDee narrowed her focus even more. Zeke was up to something, but what? A disquieting thought struck her. *Oh, no, please. Not you, too, Uncle Zeke. Please don't be involved in this scheme to marry off Joshua—and especially not to—* She could not bring herself to add her name to her fear. "Why *did* you ask me to spend the summer with you?"

The color in Zeke's face suddenly drained, then his cheeks flamed red. "I told ya." He shifted his attention to the river again. "I just thought it'd be nice if we got to know each other better."

"And that's all?" DeeDee pushed him further. She was not certain she truly wanted the real answer, yet she had to know.

He lifted one shoulder. "That's enough, ain't it?"

DeeDee swallowed back her guesswork. Still, she pursued the question. "Uncle Zeke, do you know about Miss Minnie's and Miss Maisie's little matchmakin' game? You know, the one with Rebecca and Ruth Alice as the prospects for marriage with Reverend Wylie?"

Still peering out over the water, Zeke answered her with only a twitch of one brow.

She hesitated a minute. Did she really want to know the reason behind her uncle's invitation? Could she not just enjoy the summer in blissful ignorance? No. Her curiosity would not let her. "Why were you so pleased that I might like Joshua a minute ago?"

He did not answer.

"Uncle Zeke?"

"Look, DeeDee, he's a very nice man, and—he's perfect for—"

"No," she whispered her disbelief. She shook her head. He did not have to say anything more. She knew the answer. He *had* entered her in the contest.

"Oh, Uncle Zeke, you couldn't have!" She jumped to her feet.

But he leaped up and stopped her from leaving. "C'mon, DeeDee, girl."

"Don't call me that! Don't say my name!" Her face burned hot. "How could you do such a thing to me? I thought you truly liked me. I thought I was your favorite niece." She fought to pull away from him.

He gripped her by both wrists. "Hold on, now. I care 'bout ya more than ya'll ever know. You're the most important thing in my—"

"Oh, sure!" Jerking her arms down, she broke his grasp. She did not want to hear anymore. "Important enough to throw me off on the first person you think'll make a suitable husband. Is that it, Uncle Zeke? You and Father must have both laughed good and hard over *this* little scheme in your letters back and forth. And a preacher of all people! Oh, what a good choice. Father must've been ecstatic at the prospect, huh?"

"Look! I thought you'd like him—I still do." He leaned into her line of tear-filled vision, his expression sincere. "I just want ya to be happy, girl. It's time ya thought 'bout things like marriage, and children, and all. Yer gettin' a little old fer gallivantin' around and fantasizin' 'bout them dime-novel heroes and the like—"

"Oh, so now it's children, too? And I'm gettin' too old, too. How nice of you to look out for me." DeeDee stilled. Her anger spiraled. "And I thought you were different from Father. You're just like him—you and Joshua Wylie, too. I suppose *he* thinks this's hilarious." Disgusted, she waved her hands in the air. "Imagine, Rebecca and Ruth Alice all but throwin' themselves at him. And me . . . the rowdy little hellion waitin' to be tamed. I suppose he thinks I'm the funniest of them all?"

"C'mon, now, DeeDee. It's not like that."

"Oh? And just *how* is it, Uncle Zeke?" She folded her arms over her chest. "Do tell me."

He hesitated.

"Mmm-hmm, that's what I thought." Wheeling away from him, she headed back toward town.

"Wait a minute," he said, hurrying up to her. "Where do ya think ye're goin'?"

"To pack my things," she answered, stomping through the underbrush. "I'll be leavin' on the next train out of town."

"To where?" His anger seemed to match hers. "Home?"

She slowed her pace a little. No. She could not—would not go back there. So where, then? "I'm not sure—San Francisco maybe."

"And what'll ya do fer money to get there?"

DeeDee stopped in her tracks. Damnation. He was right again. She had precious little money left from her trip. She glanced up at him. No. She was not about to ask *him* for anything—not after what he had just admitted. Resuming her stride, she shrugged. "I have a little money left. I'll go as far as it'll take me, then I'll get a job to make enough to carry me through to California."

"Then what?" Zeke sounded out of breath. "Ya don't know nobody out there. Without no family, no friends, what'll ya do? Big cities like that're just teemin' with young gals like yerself. And all of 'em lookin' fer somethin' new. And where d'ya think most of 'em ends up?"

DeeDee slowed even more. He was beginning to make her doubt her intentions.

"Hell, girl, the saloons and cathouses out West're full a gals runnin' away from somethin'—mostly their own families."

"I'm not runnin' away from anythin'," she said defiantly. "I'm runnin' *to* somethin'. I know what I want."

"Really?" He stopped and stared at her. "And what's that?"

DeeDee faltered a step. She stopped, her mind whirling like a little dust devil. She had no idea what it was she wanted. And she was lying. She was not running to anything. It was like Zeke had said. So far, she had only fantasized about her future.

"Look." He moved up nose to nose with her. His voice softened. "I know you're prideful."

She chewed on her lip to hold back the tiny smile that crept up to the corners of her mouth.

"I'm sorry 'bout what I done. I truly thought you'd meet the parson and fall head-over-heels in love with him. He ain't hard to look at, ya know?" He still sounded hopeful. "And, I thought it'd teach them two ol' gals back at that boardinghouse a lesson."

His explanation only served to prick DeeDee's temper more. "Uncle Zeke, I—"

"Okay—okay!" He raised his hands defensively. "I got the picture. Ya ain't interested."

DeeDee arched a brow. *Did I say that?* She had not said that.

"How 'bout we strike up a bargain?"

She tipped her head to one side. "What kind of bargain?"

"Well, I know yer a grown woman and all now, and ya prob'ly got yer mind set on this San Francisco stuff, but I really would like the chance fer us to get to know each other a little better before ya head out." He paused as if contemplating his next words. "So how's 'bout ya go ahead and stay here—"

She opened her mouth to object.

"Just fer the first part a the summer," he rushed on. "I need someb'dy to help me with my dentistin' and barberin' and such."

"Uncle Zeke, I know what you're tryin' to do," she said accusingly.

"Now, hold on. It's true. Why, just last week I was talkin' to some of the fellas that comes into the shop, and I was tellin' 'em how I'd like to get me a second chair." He nodded. "Truth is, with the train comin' through and all, and with so many people, I got more business sometimes than I can handle. 'Specially durin' the hot months. And ever'body always gets so persnickety when they can't get their hair snipped or a bad tooth yanked right away."

"So why not take in a partner?"

"That's what I'm gettin' at."

"But I told you, I don't want to stay. I want to—"

"I know—I know. Just hear me out."

DeeDee held any further protests in reserve. She was curious as to what he was up to now.

"You know how to cut hair. You could work fer me until I could find a real barber. Hell, the men'll prob'ly love havin' a woman fer a barber."

"Mmm-hmm, and what about their wives? Most of the women in town already hate me."

"Now, that ain't true." Zeke smiled. He slipped one huge arm around her shoulders, then wheeled them back toward Harmony. "They just don't know ya. Hell, maybe some a them'll even come in fer—"

"What?" DeeDee chuckled sarcastically. "A haircut?"

"Well, I don't know." He waved a hand helplessly. "Ya never can tell."

DeeDee snorted. "Sure they might." She knew he was really looking to keep her with him for as long as he could. And he was just using the prospect of increasing business as a means to do so.

"Well, then, that's it." He grinned. The sparkle in his eyes turned frosty blue. "We'll make up a sign today, announcin' things, and put it in the window fer tomorrow."

Clutching him around his waist, DeeDee decidedly cast away her anger and gave in to her need to be close to her uncle. Although it had never made any sense to her as to why she should, she did love this man dearly—loved him with a fierceness she could never explain—not even to herself.

He was funny and gentle, forceful and determined when it was necessary, as he had been earlier when he had come after her from the church. And he always seemed to understand her—even when she did not understand herself. And though he had not been around much while she was growing up, he was the epitome of the fantasy father Aaron Gallagher could never be. She and Zeke were so much alike that sometimes it felt as if they had both been carved from the same hunk of wood.

She did want to go to San Francisco—someday. But it touched her heart to think that Zeke would go to so much trouble and come up with such a scheme to keep her with him a little while longer. For the moment it did not matter that it was just a device to keep her in Harmony.

Her conscience dug into her momentary joy. *And what if the real reason he wants to keep you here is just so you'll be nearby Joshua Wylie? What if he still wants to try and match you two up?*

DeeDee reflected on the question. Zeke's earlier words about the minister moved in on her mind.

*"He ain't hard to look at."*

No. It was not hard to look at Joshua Wylie. It was very easy, even a little delightful, though at times a bit unnerving. She blushed at the consideration. As if she thought her uncle might be able to read her mind, she glanced up at Zeke.

Of course, he had not noticed anything.

She relaxed and leaned into his embrace. Yeah, so what if his business ploy was just part of an elaborate ruse to keep her near Joshua? She would just have to keep herself aware of what was going on at all times. And she would not let herself get hooked into her uncle's game. She would stay and earn enough money for her trip and then . . . ? Who knew?

Sunday worship was just letting out as she and Zeke entered the street in front of the boardinghouse.

Reverend Wylie stood on the top landing of the church, shaking hands with the parishioners as they took their departures.

DeeDee cut a furtive glance toward the young minister.

As if he suddenly sensed her presence, he, too, peered out at her.

Feeling a momentary shudder of excitement, she smiled. *Yessir, Uncle Zeke, Joshua Wylie certainly is easy to look at. Of that, there's no denying. But marriage?*

For the briefest of moments she allowed herself to ponder the idea. She could almost envision herself standing next to him, smiling and shaking hands with the congregation. *Hmm. I could do worse. And he does have the potential of being a really fine minister. Especially with the right kind of influence.*

One behind the other, Rebecca Ellen Russell and Ruth Alice Orndorff stepped forward and accepted Joshua's hand in greeting.

DeeDee felt the hairs on the back of her neck suddenly stand at attention. She was instantly envious of them enjoying his touch. Her eyes narrowed on the women.

They were both very attractive. And each had deep-rooted religious qualities befitting a reverend's wife. And both were just as proper as fresh-washed underwear, but they displayed no real life, no spark of excitement with which to inspire Joshua in his duties as a minister.

She arched a brow and smiled to herself. *Yes, well, as far as considering either of those two for marriage, Joshua Wylie, you could do a lot worse than me, too.*

♥♥ *Chapter 8*

EARLY THE NEXT morning Joshua awoke feeling as bright and cheerful as the sun-kissed Kansas day stretching its golden-pink fingers of light in through his window. Today he would start to build his own house. His heart picked up an excited pace.

When he had been left as a child at the orphanage, a twenty-dollar gold piece had been found tucked inside the blankets bundling him. Reverend Harkington had taken the money and put it into a bank savings.

Over the years it had grown from the interest into a modest but adequate sum. The old minister had said it should be used for something special, something just for Joshua. And for Joshua, that something special was a house of his own. After waiting weeks for the funds to arrive, he had finally received them.

Slipping on a blue cotton workshirt, he crossed his room and peered down at the street below. The roadway remained empty, but the businesses had already begun stirring to life.

Joshua shifted his gaze across to where Jake Sutherland was just opening the great doors to the livery.

Abby Lee Sutherland stood holding out a bunch of carrots to one of the horses in the corral.

Spotting her, Jake looked around, then eased up and grabbed her from behind.

She let out a little shriek.

Joshua smiled. He could not help but chuckle at the blacksmith's antics.

Jake turned his wife around in his arms and kissed her long and fully. Then, as one, clutching each other around the waist, the couple turned toward the livery and disappeared inside.

Joshua sighed reflectively. How nice it must be to have someone to share your life in that way. Pushing his shirt buttons through their matching holes, he found himself wishing he were as lucky as Jake Sutherland.

He tucked the shirttail into his pants. How long would it be until he found someone as endearing to bring completion to his existence? He walked back to the other side of the room and sat on the end of the bed. Picking up a workboot, he slipped it on his foot, allowing his mind to tread deeper into the thought, creating the illusive woman that might someday share his name.

A shadow moved through the recesses of his mind, and, with each second, it breezed nearer, becoming more distinct. Heavenly eyes like sky-blue satin wavered into the light, beckoning him to give himself up to their commands.

Tugging on a leather shoelace, he smiled and shook his head. Daydreams were nice, but he had to get to dressed if he was going to get started on his house today.

*I am here, Joshua. See me now and know I am here,* the voiceless call of the woman beckoned him.

His body stirred. His fingers stilled on the shoe-strings.

Rich auburn hair, long and vibrant, tumbling over slender shoulders like autumn leaves drifting down from tree branches, formed around a high-spirited face.

He shuddered, longing to run his hands through the lengthy mass. Who was she? He could not see her clearly.

A clattering of cans rattled outside.

He blinked, and the vision disappeared. He shivered in the wake of its fading. He gave himself a mental shrug. It was just as well. He did not have the time to spend on such nonsense. He shoved his other foot inside the remaining workboot, fumbled it tied, then walked to the window and peered out again.

Clad in a pair of men's buckskin britches and a denim shirt, DeeDee Gallagher was just crossing the street from the mercantile carrying four capped buckets of what looked to be paint.

What was she up to? His mind reverted to his earlier reverie. The vision appeared again. The imaginary woman's auburn hair forming around DeeDee's face. Joshua swallowed. No. It was just a fantasy. She could not have been the likeness he had seen. . . .

He watched her until she moved in front of the barbershop and he could no longer see her. He suddenly had to know what she was up to with all that paint. Hurrying from the room, he dashed down the stairs and out into the daylight.

"Miss DeeDee," Joshua called out once he had secured the door to the boardinghouse closed behind him.

She looked up, but continued to pry open the lids to the cans.

"Is that paint?"

"Yes."

"What're you planning to do with it, repaint Zeke's shop?"

"Mmm-hmm." She kept her focus trained on her chore.

"Really?" Joshua turned down his collar as he approached her. "Does Lillie Taylor know about this?"

DeeDee snorted loudly. "Does she need to?"

Joshua held his mouth to a taut smile. This was not going to go over well. Apparently, DeeDee did not know about Lillie Taylor's Beautification Committee. "Didn't Zeke tell you about her?"

DeeDee lifted her gaze to his. "No. Why?"

Should he tell her? He had to. She did not need any more trouble with the town. And Lord help her when Lillie Taylor and the other women on the committee saw that she had changed their *glorious color scheme*. He had to warn her that they would not be pleased.

"Look, Miss DeeDee—"

"I thought we decided my name was just DeeDee—without the Miss."

"Mmm—yes." He did not want to go through that again. "DeeDee, does your uncle know you're doing this?"

She shook her head and smiled pridefully. "No, it's my gift to him." She sank a stick into one of the open containers, stirred it a couple of seconds, then lifted it, exposing the dripping yellow paint from the can. "It's Uncle Zeke's favorite color. It's sorta temper'ry, but we're goin' into business together. So I thought I'd git up early and git started—ya know—surprise him with a show of my 'preciation. That way he cain't say no."

Joshua shook his head. She was using that frontier dialect again. "I thought we were past your needing to use that common speech with me."

She did not answer, just went on about her job as if she had not heard him.

He hesitated another moment. "You just might want to talk to Zeke before you go to all this—"

"I told you, Reverend—"

"I thought we decided on Joshua. No Reverend, just Joshua." He grinned.

Her cheeks turned a delightful shade of pink. She glanced down, then looked back at him, with a subtle smile. "Yes, well, I told you, *Joshua*, it's a surprise." She stared at him another moment before returning to her work.

He thought about pursuing the matter further, but relented. What good would it do? It was only too apparent that DeeDee intended on going through with her *painting surprise* no matter what the outcome.

He watched her slap on the first strokes of paint. Then, after another few minutes, he stepped backward, and wheeled around. He plunged forward. Quick to react, he caught himself gripping the edges of the trough with his hands. His startled reflection stared up at him from the water.

Behind him, DeeDee giggled.

Shooting her a backward glance, he straightened.

"Better watch that thing, Joshua." She smiled sweetly. "I think it's startin' to take a special likin' to you."

Brushing his palms together, Joshua chuckled with a nod. "You know? I think you're right."

DeeDee saluted him with a brush-in-hand wave, then returned to her job.

It took nearly an hour and a half for Joshua to load the materials he had ordered from the mercantile the previous week onto a buckboard he had borrowed from the livery and deliver them down to the site he had picked out. Behind the church and off to one side, he removed the lumber, nails, and various tools he had purchased.

By noon, he had already put down the floor atop the previously prepared bottom supports of his house. He had long since removed his shirt, and now worked diligently with only his suspendered pants and boots for cover against the sun's interminable heat.

Holding on to a mouthful of nails with his teeth, he toe-nailed a corner brace into place. How many days would it take to complete his house? Miss Maisie and Miss Minnie were congenial, and their cooking was as notably tasty as any celebrated restaurant, but still it was not *his* home. He could hardly wait to finish his project and move in. Then, and only then, would he truly feel a part of the community. He couldn't really explain why he'd turned down all offers to help from his congregation. He knew the house could be built in a day or two and be turned into a town event, but he really just wanted to do it himself. With his background, he just didn't believe it could be real unless he measured every board and hammered every nail himself.

A shadow passed above him, then a pair of Indian moccasins moved into view.

He glanced up, sweat trickling in his eyes. Rising to a sitting position on his knees, he blinked and wiped the moisture away with his forearm. He squinted up at the woman smiling in front of him.

Her face dappled with yellow paint, DeeDee Gallagher held up a red-checkered-napkin bundle.

"When I went in for lunch, I noticed you weren't there. Uncle Zeke told me you was—were over here workin', so I brought you a couple of sandwiches." She looked around at his morning accomplishment and nodded with obvious approval. "So this's what all that pounding I've been hearing's for."

Joshua jumped up and moved to retrieve his shirt.

"Oh, that's okay. You don't have to put that on on my account. I've been around men working without their shirts before."

Joshua furrowed his brows. She had?

"I mean, I do have a father and a couple of brothers," she stated, as if she had read his mind.

"Oh," he said flatly. Funny, besides Zeke, he had never before considered any thoughts of her family. "So what did Zeke think of your surprise?" He had to know what had happened when the barber saw his shop.

"He just laughed." DeeDee shrugged. "I thought he was laughing at me at first, but then he assured me he wasn't. He mumbled something about the Ladies' Auxiliary and some Beautification Committee, and he just laughed again. Said he liked it, though, and somethin' about if it had been his choice, he'd have painted it that color in the first place."

Joshua chuckled. He knew exactly what the man was talking about. The ladies of Harmony were more than likely going to bluster through town with all the anger and fury of a summer cyclone. It was a wonder they had not started already.

"It's chicken," DeeDee said.

"Excuse me?" he said, opening the napkin bundle and removing one of the sandwiches.

"Your lunch." She pointed to the slices of bread. "It's chicken, left over from last night's supper."

He glanced down at the meal she had brought him.

"You don't mind leftover chicken, do you?"

"No, I love it. Have you eaten?"

"Yep. Just finished." She gestured for him to sit. "You go ahead."

"Will you join me in a moment of thanks?" Without waiting for a reply, he bowed his head. "For what we are about to receive, oh Lord, we are truly grateful. Amen." It was not as grand and lengthy as either Miss Minnie's or Miss Maisie's prayers, but he was certain the Almighty understood his intent—moreover, enjoyed his brevity.

Plopping down on the edge of the flooring, DeeDee handed him a Mason jar of cold lemonade. "Uncle Zeke tells me you're buildin' you a house back here."

"Mmm-hmm," he answered around a mouthful. He chewed a few times and swallowed. "I've saved a little money over the years. Now that I've been assigned to my own parish, I figure it's time I built me a home of my own and settled down."

"And doesn't that just fit in with everybody's plans," she said in a flip tone.

Joshua chomped down on another bite. "What?" He crunched the food between his teeth, swallowed again, then cleared his throat. "What did you say?"

She shrugged. "Oh, nothin'." Standing, she stepped up onto the floor and walked from area to area, as if she were strolling through the finished house. "Parlor. Kitchen. Pantry. Is this a bedroom?" Frowning, she peered up from one end of the footage.

He shook his head, then took a sip of lemonade to wash down another bite of food. "No. That's going to be my study."

Her expression still etched with a perplexed scowl, she set her hands atop her hips and looked around at the area. "So where's the bedroom?" Tipping her head to one side, she shot him a baffled stare. "You *do* plan on sleeping some time, don't you?"

Laughing, Joshua wiped his mouth on the napkin, then set the bundle down on the floor. He stepped up onto the wood platform, then moved to where she stood. He pointed skyward. "The bedroom'll be upstairs."

Her face lit up like the dawning of a morning sky. She squinted off in the direction of the river. "Let me see." Dashing across the floor, she hurried to the buckboard and retrieved the ladder still lying in the back of the wagon.

"What on earth are you doing?" he asked, moving to her aid.

"I want to see," she answered, motioning for him to set up the ladder in the middle of his proposed study.

"See what?" For the life of him he could not decipher her reasoning.

Once the ladder was set up, DeeDee scurried up to the top, shielded her eyes from the sun with her hand, and peered out over the landscape at the back of the house. She held up her hands as if she was holding a large picture frame. "Oh, it's perfect, Joshua. A big bay window—with a seat—and cushions right here."

A tiny tremor racked his senses. It was the first time she had ever used his name without being prompted into doing so. Instantly he realized where he had placed his hands. Without thinking, he had clutched the lower portions of her calves, supporting her in case of a fall.

"What a breathtaking sight. You can see the river, the trees, and way over there . . ."

Joshua had stopped listening. Instead, he concentrated on the taut feel of her leg muscles playing beneath the fabric of her pants against his palms. They teased his emotions, sparking a strange flicker of heat in the pit of his stomach. He thought back to his morning daydream.

*Could* she be the woman in his fantasy? Why not? She was smart, witty, and even on the one occasion when they had argued, he had found that he had still enjoyed being with her. And she was wonderful with children.

His gaze shifted, traveling up the full length of her backside. Oh, Lord, children. He was completely captivated by the glorious sight of each and every curve. She looked like she was built just for the purpose of bearing many beautiful children. He could just imagine a little girl with sparkling blue eyes and a curly crop of auburn hair just like her mother's. And two or three strapping sons—

"Joshua? You goin' to make me stay up here all day?"

Startled, he blinked. He looked up to where she stared down at him over her shoulder.

Wide, expressive eyes peered down at him through a splattering of paint.

Heaven help him, even yellow-speckled, she was beautiful. Yes, it was possible. She could very well be the woman in his fantasy. He peered deeper. Who could say what would happen if they got to know each other? Only God knew the answer to these things.

"Joshua?"

"O-oh, I, uh—I beg your pardon," he stuttered. He lowered his hands and quickly stepped backward.

Turning around on the ladder, she smiled, nearly hopping from one rung to the next as she made her hasty descent. "I do have a barbershop to finish— ohhh!" DeeDee's pant leg caught on a protruding nail in the ladder. The fabric ripped. She lost her balance.

Joshua tried to brace her with his arms.

She plunged downward, landing full-force against his face and chest.

Together, they toppled backward, thudding against the planked floor.

The ladder barely missed the two of them as it, too, hit the platform.

DeeDee's breath rushed out against his forehead.

Joshua groaned with the weight of her body slamming against his. The back of his head smacked the floor hard. Stunned for a moment, he did not move. After taking a second to gather his wits, he peered up at DeeDee.

Large, saucer-shaped eyes stared at him from only inches away. "You okay?"

He stretched an arm. Her shirt moved against his bare skin. Her warmth penetrated her clothing, searing his chest. Of their own volition, his fingers fanned her spine, just above her hips. He inhaled sharply.

Her sun-heated body filled his sense of smell. Closing his eyes, his nostrils flared, reveling in the pure womanly scent of her. He had never before been this close—this intimate with a woman. His body came to life beneath her touch.

"Joshua," she asked timidly. "Are you okay?"

He opened his eyes and looked up at her. Hovering just above him, her lips taunted his restraint. "No," he replied without thinking.

"Oh, my good Lord!" She pushed herself up, her braced arms stretched above either side of his shoulders. "Did I hurt you?"

"Yes." He was not thinking still, only reacting. It was not a lie. He felt genuine pain from her lying fully atop him, though it was not a true injury, more like an immediate and intense agony. The force of it felt as if it might tear him in half.

"You stay right here," she said in a fearful whisper. "I'll go get help." Though she kept her upper body elevated as before, she pushed off him.

He gripped her tighter.

Her breath caught. She froze, a curious expression sweeping her features as she stared down at him.

Neither spoke. Their gazes met.

Raw emotion shone in her eyes, darkening their color to a steel-blue. Her breathing quickened. Her heartbeat pounded against Joshua's chest. Or was that his own?

Boldly he reached up to her face, and brushed aside an errant strand of hair that had escaped her plaited locks. It was as if some unseen entity had taken control of his actions. He did not try to stop it. It felt too good, too exciting. His gaze lowered to her lips. He wanted to kiss her, to know their warmth, their softness, the taste of her.

"Oh, my! Oh, my!" A familiar voice attacked his hearing from the near-distance.

Instantly they both looked up.

Rebecca Ellen Russell stood staring at them from the back corner of the church.

With a gasp, DeeDee lunged to her feet.

Joshua rolled over and pushed himself up to a standing position. He darted a nervous glance at DeeDee.

She returned the look.

"Ah, Miss Rebecca." How would he explain this? He had to think fast. "You're just in time."

Wide-eyed, Rebecca stared at the two of them. She shifted her weight from foot to foot with fretful movements. "Just in time for what?"

Joshua looked around, searching for a creative way of interpreting what she had witnessed. He spied the tear in DeeDee's pants, and saw the deep scrape showing through the rip. "Why, to help DeeDee back to the boardinghouse." He shot a furtive glance at DeeDee, then nodded down at her leg, mentally suggesting she go along with his ploy.

"Oh, yeah." She backed over to the toppled ladder and sat down on its side. "I fell, and I—"

"She scraped her shin on a nail," Joshua said, moving closer and kneeling beside her. He looked back at Rebecca. "It's bleeding. On second thought, could you run to the doctor's office and get some antiseptic? We don't want this to get infected."

Rebecca remained trancelike another second before finally nodding. "Is it bad?"

"Not too. I think if we can just get some medication and maybe a bandage on it, she'll be fine," Joshua told the dark-haired woman.

"I see," she said in a voice that bespoke total belief of his story. She whipped around, but halted mid-stride, and dashed over to the edge of the planking. She set a basket on one corner. "I forgot. Here's your lunch, Joshua. Miss Minnie thought you might be hungry."

He gestured his thanks with a smile and a nod.

Obvious pleasure marking her little-girl features, Rebecca batted her eyes, her mouth drawing into a small grin. Then, wheeling away from them, she hurried in the direction of the church.

DeeDee sighed with an audible breath.

Joshua looked up at her.

Their gazes locked, silently reviewing the whirlwind emotions of a moment ago.

Flitting a glance downward, DeeDee pulled her
injured leg up and inspected it more thoroughly. "I
didn't even feel it." She shot a nervous glance to his
face, before returning her attention to her leg. She
pulled up the fabric. "I really don't think it's bad
enough for a bandage, though."

Joshua moved closer for a better look at her
injury. "I had to tell her something to get her to
leave."

DeeDee looked at him again.

Joshua's blood heated. His pulse leaped to a
quicker pace. Captivated by her eyes, he did not
move. He did not dare, for God help him, he might
try to kiss her again.

"I should go." DeeDee's voice quavered just
above a whisper.

Could it be that she felt the same as he? Could
she be as interested in him as he was in her? And
could it also be that she, too, was as excited by him
as he was by her? A new boldness crept into his
being. He had to know for certain.

Hesitantly, he touched her fingertips.

She did not encourage his actions, but neither did
she obstruct his advance.

With daring determination, he slipped his palm
atop the back of her hand.

She did not flinch. Her gaze clung to his.

"DeeDee?" Zeke called out from somewhere in
the direction of the barbershop.

She blinked. "It's Uncle Zeke," she said, sounding a bit out of breath, maybe even a little frightened. She shoved his hand away with the quick push-down of her pant leg. "I—I've got to get—to get back." She suddenly appeared flustered.

"What's wrong?"

She looked as though she had just been caught committing some heinous act. "I just have to get back, that's all," she repeated, jumping to her feet. Before he could move to stop her, she dashed across the flooring.

"DeeDee, wait," Joshua called after her.

"Tell Rebecca I went back over to the shop to finish painting," she called over her shoulder. "Would you ask her to bring the antiseptic to me over there?"

"But, DeeDee—"

"Thanks for showin' me the plans to your house, Joshua. See you later," she hollered, a note of forced nonchalance in her voice. She disappeared around the corner of the church.

Joshua stared after her for a long time before he finally went back to work. He was baffled. Why had she reacted so strangely when Zeke had called her? She had not done anything wrong. She had just brought him lunch.

His mind tortured him with questions. *But that's not all you did.*

After regathering his tools, Joshua returned to his chore. He had a lot to ponder. He had touched DeeDee's hand. He had held her atop him after the fall, and she had not resisted. And if they had not been interrupted by Rebecca, he more than likely *would* have kissed her. Would she have thwarted that contact? He would like to think that she would not. Still. He sighed. He had a lot to think about—a lot to consider.

It was nearly four o'clock when Joshua finally stopped for the day. He would not have quit then, except for the burning pain that seared the flesh on his back. He knew he had to be sunburned pretty badly. He could feel the scorching heat stinging his skin.

Taking his shirt, he gingerly put it on. The soft fabric bit into his flesh. He had been so involved with his work, moreover with his thoughts of DeeDee, that he had not considered the strength of the sun's burning rays. He grimaced. He should have been more careful.

After putting away his tools, he delivered the buckboard back to the livery, then ambled home. Upon his approach to the boardinghouse, he looked for DeeDee. The cans were still out, but she was nowhere to be seen.

"Ya lookin' fer somebody, Parson?" Zeke called to him from just inside his shop.

Joshua shook his head. "I was just wondering how far DeeDee got on her painting today."

"Oh, she's around back." Zeke indicated her location with a wave of his hand. He shook his head and chuckled. "That girl's somethin', ain't she?"

"Pardon me?" What had the man meant by that? Could it be that Zeke had seen Joshua and DeeDee together earlier?

"I mean with this paintin' and all. Says she ain't quittin' till she gets it finished."

Joshua studied the thorough job she had done on the front of the building. She was definitely no slouch when it came to working. He glanced around. "Has anyone else said anything about her changing the color?" He peered at the older man, indicating his meaning with vaulted brows.

"Ohhh, yeah," Zeke said. Chuckling, he gripped his suspenders, rocking back and forth from his toes to his heels. He nodded toward the boardinghouse. "Matter-a-factly, that there Ladies' Auxiliary is holdin' their weekly meetin' right now." His expression sobered. "Prob'ly pullin' out every feather in their ruffled little bodies tryin' to figger out what to do 'bout DeeDee and all this paint."

Joshua flinched. His back was beginning to really sting. He had to get out of these clothes and put something on his sunburn and fast.

"I gotta admit, Parson," Zeke continued. "I sure am interested as to what they're plannin'. I been hearin' their flustered cacklin' all afternoon, and it's got my curiosity rankled sorely."

"Yes." Joshua grimaced against the searing pain on his back. "I can understand that."

"You all right?"

Joshua nodded. "At least, I will be as soon as I get upstairs and take care of this sunburn."

"Yeah, I figgered that would happen right off when I seen ya out there workin' without yer shirt." He gestured down the street with a wave of his hand. "Doc's prob'bly got some salve that'll help ya some."

Doctor. The word tweaked Joshua's memory. "Oh, yes. Did Rebecca ever get DeeDee the antiseptic for her leg?"

Ezekiel shrugged. "I guess that's what she brought her. DeeDee said she scratched up her leg some." He frowned, then stared at Joshua with a puzzled look. "How'd you know?"

The pain in Joshua's back demanded his attention. "I'll go on in and see what I can find out," he said, edging toward the boardinghouse. "I have to get this shirt off." Then, without waiting, he wheeled fully around and headed for the door.

He did not mean to appear rude, but the pain was becoming more and more unbearable. And, too, he was worried about the intentions of the Ladies' Auxiliary. He knew DeeDee could handle herself in most predicaments, but Lillie Taylor might be a bit too much for even DeeDee to handle.

He could hear them talking when he entered the house.

"She's only been here for a few days," Lillie Taylor was saying, "and just look at everything she's done. Why, on her very first day alone, she nearly drowned the poor Reverend. Then she tried to impose her wretched voice on our choir."

"Now, Lillie. That's not entirely true," Zan Winchester interjected. "Ed told me that it was Zeke that wanted her to join the church choir. Ed said this Delilah didn't even act like she wanted to be there."

"Well, be that as it may, if it were up to me, I'd have her run clean out of town. Changing the color scheme I worked so hard on shows a true lack of respect."

Joshua quietly closed the door behind him, then moved across the large vestibule to the stairs. That way if he were to be caught in the house, it would look like he was just returning from his work and going up to his room. He silently crept up a couple of steps, then stopped to listen further.

"I don't think we need to do anything quite that drastic." It was Nancy Tolliver who spoke this time. "Did anyone actually tell DeeDee about the Beautification Committee?"

No one spoke. Apparently no one had told DeeDee.

"You know, it *is* Zeke's shop," Mrs. Lind reminded the women. "And DeeDee *is* his niece. She really doesn't have to ask anyone else's permission but his."

"Zeke Gallagher agreed to the decision of our committee a long time ago," Lillie Taylor argued. "If he didn't like the color we chose for his shop, he should have said so then."

Joshua shot a glance heavenward. As if anyone had ever had a chance to argue with *that* woman.

"I think it's simply appalling and unfeeling to commit such an offense," Lillie continued. "Why, it's as if she's slapping each of our faces with one haughty blow."

"I for one agree," someone else interjected. "Why, after that—that Sunday school class she taught yesterday, my children are running around acting like a band of banshees."

"Mine, too."

Listening to the women's complaints, Joshua groaned. *Heaven help us all now.* He had been afraid everyone would find out about DeeDee's unorthodox form of teaching before he had a chance to speak to her about it privately. Not that he did not enjoy her teaching himself, nor that he thought it was wrong. On the contrary. He had loved it. And so had the children, if what he had witnessed of their behavior had been any indication.

"I think we ought to speak to Reverend Wylie about her," Lillie Taylor suggested. "I understand it was he that wanted the young woman to take Rebecca's place."

"Take Rebecca's place!" Maisie all but shrieked.

That was it! Joshua had heard enough. He had to talk to DeeDee soon. He had to warn her that she would most likely come up against some of the more discontented women of Harmony. Now, however, might not be the best time to approach her with this information. For once she knew, and discovered that the women were, at that moment, in the boardinghouse, she might very well proceed to attack them with one of those frontier tirades she was known for. No, now might not be the best time. He would wait for a safer time to talk to her.

Crossing the landing at the head of the stairs, Joshua halted just outside his room. It was apparent that *somebody* definitely needed to set the good Christian folks of Harmony on the path to understanding and forgiveness before something dreadful happened. And somewhere deep inside him, Joshua had a feeling he knew exactly who that *somebody* would turn out to be.

# ♥ ♥ Chapter 9

NEAR MIDNIGHT DEEDEE finally finished painting Zeke's barbershop. She had missed dinner, but she did not care; she was not hungry, only tired. She looked down at her yellow-speckled hands and forearms. Now, if she could just remove all these spots with the turpentine she had bought at the mercantile. Standing beneath the shop sign, she pried open the can of cleaner.

Instantly the strong pine-scent assailed her nostrils.

Wrinkling her nose, she flinched. "Oh, doesn't that just tantalize the senses?" She waved her hand as if she thought the meager effort would thwart the pungent aroma. Briefly she weighed the difference between the two. "Well, DeeDee, what's it goin' to be? To stink or to look like you're diseased?"

There was no other way of shedding the paint short of scrubbing the flesh off her body with a hard-bristled wash brush. She winced. No, that definitely did not sound very appealing.

Hesitating only another minute, she raised her hands and wiggled her fingers over the mouth of the can. She sighed. "To stink," she stated as if she were truly in agony. Cringing, she plunged her hands into the thick, oily solution, and groaned.

Like tiny, painless pinpricks, it tingled her skin.

She rubbed and scoured, scraped and scratched at the paint with her fingernails, until all of the yellow had either dissolved or flaked away. After wiping off the thick residue of turpentine from her arms, she gathered the brushes and remaining paint, then took them into Zeke's shop for safekeeping until morning.

Worn out and completely fatigued, DeeDee yawned, and stretched. She was so tired, she could hardly keep her eyes open. Absently she cupped her face with her hands, rubbing across her eyes and cheeks. "Ooo." She grimaced at the overpowering scent lingering on her skin.

Something else grabbed her attention. Stroking the contours of her face, she felt tiny splotches. What were they? Moving in front of one of the mirrors in the barbershop, she looked at her reflection and groaned. More paint. She glanced at the can of turpentine she had just set in the corner and shuddered.

"Oh, no. I'm not putting *that* stuff on *my* face."

But what was she going to use to remove the specks of yellow stain? She looked around the various shelves. Surely her uncle had *something* that would do the trick.

Reading the different stickers, she finally came across a dark blue bottle labeled White Lily Face Wash. She nodded to herself, as she read the ingredients and instructions for general use. "Well, it says *face wash*," she said, convincing herself that the clear liquid was just the thing to take care of her problem. Now, all she needed was some water.

She would like nothing better than to go up to bed, but she was not about to wake up to a yellow-tinged face, either, not to mention the overwhelming aroma of the turpentine. With a sleepy smile, she thought of the river and sighed. Yes, bed would be nice, but for now, clean came first. She could not bear the thought of enduring the oily stench a minute longer. She had to get it off of her.

Crossing the interior of the shop, she peered out at the empty street in front of the building. It was late. And there was nobody else awake. Did she dare take a chance on a bath? She shrugged. Might as well take care of everything at once.

Searching out a small soft-bristled brush, she then located a towel, a comb, a bar of soap, and another bottle containing lavender-scented shampoo. She could already feel her hands turning dry and rough from the turpentine, so she grabbed up a jar of Witch Hazel Glycerine Jelly, too. Then, after one last glance up and down the street in front of the shop, she headed outside, toward the sound of the flowing current.

She decided to go to the spot on the outskirts of town where she and Zeke had talked Sunday morning. The water was calm there. And even if someone were up and about, the chances of them stumbling across her taking a bath were pretty slim.

Setting herself up beneath the lone willow tree by the water's edge, DeeDee kept a watchful eye out for any trespassers. For all of her constant display of bravado, she had to admit she was more than a little uncomfortable at completely stripping down and exposing herself to the eyes of nature.

Still, it needed to be done. She would not give the townspeople of Harmony even one more thing to ridicule her for—even something as insignificant as yellow paint speckles. Once she had removed her clothing, she cautiously peered around the tree.

All remained as quiet as when she had first arrived.

Staying on her guard, she quickly darted out from cover and dashed into the chilly stream. Her breath slammed against her chest. The water felt colder than it had when she had gone swimming with the children a few days earlier.

"Oh, my good Lord in heaven!" she squealed. On impulse she clutched her arms over her breasts for warmth. She gritted her teeth and sank an inch or two at a time, until she was immersed to her neck. Shivering, she remained still and waited for the water touching her to be warmed by the heat of her body. But every time she moved even slightly, a swirl of cold would rush in and attack her senses.

There was no hope for comfort. She would simply have to hold on to herself and get it over with. She tilted her head back and soaked her hair. Squeezing her eyes closed, she shuddered. The cold was definitely getting the better of her. Still, she had to finish.

The soft murmur of the breeze picked up, cooling her wet skin even more. "Oh, wonderful." Her teeth began to chatter. This would never do. She would have to finish her bath quickly, or she was certain she would shake to death.

Careful to keep herself below the surface, she moved to the small sand spit where she had left her toiletries. Taking the soap and brush first, she lathered the bristles and scrubbed her face. Once she felt certain she was free of all the paint splotches, she finished the rest of her bath in rapid procession. She had to get out of the water. With the stirring of the breeze, she could not withstand the chill any longer. Her hair would simply have to wait until she was dried and dressed.

Fully clothed again, DeeDee took a few minutes to sit quietly huddled within the warmth of her own arms, allowing her body to regain its normal temperature before setting out to wash her hair. She had no desire to get wet again anytime too soon.

When the gooseflesh on her arms finally smoothed, she moved to a more comfortable position. Knees bent, she clasped her arms around them, and relaxed against the trunk of the tree.

Gazing out at the river, she watched the reflection of the full moon dance across the rippling surface of the water. How peaceful it was here. The silent lull of the stars, the soft gurgle of the current, the serenade of crickets. She sighed with contentment. If given the chance, a person could definitely learn to like it here.

Her thoughts moved along with the moon's glow that was mirrored in the river. What a tease it was to taunt the surface of the water with its gleam. How lonely the river appeared just now. Dark and haunting, it seemed to beckon the white sphere to come down and sink the heavenly light within the current's inky depths. But, instead, the moon remained high, flirting and teasing, touching yet not.

Within the gentle flow of the water, DeeDee envisioned Joshua Wylie's image wavering beneath its depths. Her own reflection suddenly illuminated within the circular white cast undulating atop the surface. Did *he* ever think of *her* like that? She was certain he knew of the contest to see him married to either Ruth Alice, Rebecca, or now, as she had discovered, her.

The whole town appeared to be in on the game, sniggling and chuckling whenever any of the contenders were found in conversation with the minister. But who did *he* want? She had not

witnessed any real display of interest from Joshua
with either of the other two women. Could it be
as Zeke had suggested? Could Joshua Wylie really
find *her* attractive? Could she truly have a chance
to be his wife?

She thought of the accident with the ladder earlier that afternoon. If Rebecca had not entered upon
the scene like she had, DeeDee felt certain Joshua
would have kissed her. She had seen his desire
shimmering in his lusterous brown eyes.

Her memory stirred with the thought of his
urgent hands pressing against her back. All day,
she had fought to keep the incident in the back
of her mind, but it had managed to creep into her
thoughts more and more. Now, alone, she battled
it no longer. She closed her eyes, summoning the
moment.

His touch had felt so warm, so right in its gentle
appeal, that she had not wanted him to release her.
As it had then, her heart fluttered, her breathing
quickened, and her body heated. She had known
his bold actions to be immoral, her own unchar-
acteristic hesitancy to be a sign of invitation, yet
she had not had the strength to pull away from
him. Lord help her, she could not lie to herself.
She had wanted him, too. Briefly, she wondered
what it would be like to share those feelings with
him on a daily basis.

With a groan of realization, she shook her head.
*What are you thinking? You're going to San
Francisco, remember? You want adventure, and
a chance to live a full life. How exciting could it*

*be to be married to a minister?*

Chuckling at her own childish fantasy, she rose up on her knees and moved the couple of feet necessary to reach the water. Time was drawing later by the minute. If she was going to wash her hair and get any rest before morning, she had better get it done. She did not relish going to sleep with wet hair, but if she wanted any sleep at all tonight, she would have to endure the chill. Facedown, she bent toward the water and dunked her head again.

As before, the cold gnashed at her scalp.

She shuddered. Then, groping for the shampoo, she poured an ample amount into her hair and scrubbed. Once she had finished rinsing, she leaned back and toweled it dry, then set about combing out the tangles.

"Enjoying the night air?"

DeeDee froze. She knew that voice. Shifting, she looked up into Joshua Wylie's all too familiar face. "What—" A lump formed in her throat, and she swallowed it back. "What're you doin' out here so late?"

"I could ask you the same thing," he answered with an arched brow. Then, holding out a towel of his own, he gestured toward the cloth draping her lap. "But I can see we both came here for the same reason."

Inwardly DeeDee shivered. He was going to take a bath? Here? Now? In the same water she had just bathed in? Strangely, the idea excited her, yet unnerved her even more. She grabbed her towel and reached for her toiletries. "I guess I'll be goin', then."

"That's not necessary." He stepped toward her, his unbuttoned shirt stirring in the light rustle of air.

Shocked at his boldness, DeeDee stared up at him. Her gaze wandered across the shade and light casting over his bare chest and stomach. She gulped back a sudden rush of anxiety. "Surely you don't mean it's okay if I stay here while you—uh—" She cleared her throat and sent a nervous glance toward the water.

"Oh, no." Obviously he had understood her meaning. He squatted down beside her and smiled. "I took my bath a little while ago." He nodded a ways down the river. "Back there."

Hesitantly she followed his line of direction with a slow, sidelong glance. That meant it was quite probable they had both been in the water . . . bathing . . . naked . . . at the same time. Like fireflies storming her stomach, that strange fluttering sensation suddenly returned.

"Actually, it was more like a soak," he said, picking a cottony seed-top of a dandelion. He twirled it in the breeze, watching the tiny fuzz-umbrellas take off in flight.

"A soak?" She stared at him in wonder. "This late at night? And in *that* cold water?"

He nodded and smiled. "It worked a miracle on my back." He arched up straight, his expression twitching from taut to relaxed. "But it's already hurting again, so it really didn't do—"

"What happened?" Instantly DeeDee became concerned. He had been fine when she had left him earlier that afternoon. Had he been injured somehow?

"Oh, nothing to worry about." He stretched up straight again, pain marking his features with each movement he made. "I'm afraid I was so excited about finally getting to work on my house, and the day was so nice, that I forgot how hot an early spring sun could be."

Curious, DeeDee leaned around to look at his back. "Let me see."

"It'll be all right," he insisted, though he did reach up over his shoulders and lift his shirt.

Even in the dusky-blue light of the moon, the red glare blazing across his skin glowed bright. "Oh, my God!" DeeDee leaped to her knees. Scooting up behind him, she clasped the material covering his back. "Take this off," she ordered, disturbed by what she saw.

"If you knew how much trouble I had putting it on, you wouldn't ask me to do that," he said with a pain-filled chuckle. Doing as she had requested, he groaned.

"Oh, Joshua, this is really bad." DeeDee grimaced. A large white X crisscrossed his back where he had worn his suspenders, but the rest of his flesh was seared red, and water blisters had already formed. She wanted to touch him, to soothe his pain, but she knew it would only cause him more agony if she did so. "Have you seen the doctor for this?"

Sucking in a deep breath, he stiffened, then shook his head. "It's just a sunburn. It'll be all right in a few days."

"That may be true, but it's the worst one I've *ever* seen." DeeDee could almost feel his pain in her own back. She wiggled uncomfortably. "You've got to get somethin' from the doc. You really need to have some kind of balm put on this. It could get infected."

He shrugged. "It's a little late in the evening for that right now, wouldn't you say?" Glancing at her over his shoulder, he grinned. "I don't think the doctor would like it very much if I woke him up just to treat a sunburn."

"But this's serious, Joshua." Her mind flitted toward the toiletries she had brought with her. The witch hazel jelly. "Sit down," she commanded sternly. She scurried over and retrieved the jar, then hurried back to him. "Well, it does say it's good for sunburns on the label."

"What?" Pulling his legs up into an Indian-style seat, Joshua frowned. "What's that stuff?"

"It's witch hazel," she said, reading the rest of the sticker on the glass container.

"But isn't that for your face?"

"It's for a lot of things. And it's all I've got." She unscrewed the top and took a sniff. It was lightly scented with lavender. "It claims to soothe chapped hands and ease burns."

"But—"

Sticking her fingers into the jar, she scooped out a large amount of jelly, then returned her

attention to his back. Where to touch him first?
Anywhere she applied the salve was going to hurt.
She swallowed, then took a breath. "I'll try to be
careful," she said, then gingerly smoothed it onto
one shoulder.

He flinched, but did not utter a sound.

With light, circular strokes she continued
smearing the ointment as evenly as she dared.
Traversing the ebb and flow of his brawn with her
hands, DeeDee felt those unnerving fireflies begin
to swarm in her stomach again.

Joshua Wylie was not nearly as big nor as stal-
wart as a lot of men she had seen, but then he did
not have the same job as most men. His work did
not consist of lifting heavy loads, like the workers
did with the great sacks of flour in the mill. Nor
did he pound iron into horseshoes all day like Jake
Sutherland at the livery. He did not even have to
crawl atop someone and hold them down like her
Uncle Zeke had to do when he was extracting a
tooth.

Gently, carefully, she palmed another dollop of
the thick salve over the contours of his back. With
him facing away from her, she continued to take
full advantage of studying him intimately.

No, Joshua Wylie displayed the magnitude of his
strength in less obvious manners. She thought of
the adorable way the corners of his mouth twitched
just before he was about to smile. And the way his
eyes twinkled when he looked at her.

Lowering her gaze with the movements of her
hands, she shuddered. She knew it was only the

heat of the sunburn that she felt blazing through the salve, but it excited her even so. She darted a look up to where the light wind stirred the hair against his neck. Lord help her, but she would dearly love to comb her fingers through his lengthy mane. Without thought she slid her hands steadily downward, rubbing the jelly onto his sides.

He wiggled.

Reality returned. "Sorry," she murmured.

"It's all right. It just tickled."

She smiled, for in that same stroke of time, she had felt an identical sensation dart upward from the lower region of her body, to her brain. She stilled her movements, slipping her study to where her hands remained against his back at the waistband of his pants. Startled by her own heedlessness, she jerked away her touch. "There. I rubbed it in as best I could," she said, trying to sound composed, but knowing she did not. She prayed he had not recognized her distraction as excitement. "I—uh—hope it helps."

He shuddered beneath another rustle of the breeze. "Well, even if it doesn't, I can't see where it would hurt it any—at least, any more than it already does." It was only too obvious by the way he kept wrenching every time he moved that he was still in a great deal of pain. Stretching up tall in his sitting position, he flexed the muscles across his back as he slipped his shirt back on.

DeeDee wiped the lingering ointment from her hands onto her towel, allowing her gaze to follow his movements. Still and all, she had to admit that even though Joshua was not as physically active as most men, he had a most attractive physique.

Joshua shifted around so that he now faced her.

The weightiness of his lingering stare became unbearable. She lifted her gaze from her hands to his eyes. Why was he looking at her so intently? What was he thinking? It had been one thing for her to make a close study of him when he was unaware, but *she* was only too aware of *his* consideration, and it disturbed her more than she could bear. She could not stand it any longer. She needed to get out from under his scrutiny. "Joshua—"

"DeeDee—"

They spoke the names simultaneously.

DeeDee laughed nervously.

He chuckled. "You go first."

She shook her head. "No, you." She really did not have anything to say. She just wanted to remove his attention from herself. Picking up her comb, she started to wrestle the tangles from her hair. When he did not speak, she looked up and waited, watching him with interest.

Still holding on to a pause, he glanced heavenward. Then, after a few minutes, he finally looked back at her.

Was something wrong? He suddenly appeared troubled.

"Why did you run out on my sermon yesterday?" he blurted out in a rush.

DeeDee flinched. She stopped midstroke and stared at him. How should she answer? He had been so involved in reading his sermon the previous morning that she had not considered he might have witnessed her escape from the church. Now he had her cornered.

She peered a little deeper, trying to see inside him. Could he handle the truth? She had no choice but to tell him. After that he could do with his sermons as he saw fit. But afterward, how would he feel toward her? She sighed resolutely. She would worry about that later.

"DeeDee?" His expression sharpened, then softened around his eyes. "I'd like to know what happened. If there's a problem, I'd like to help if I can."

Oh, yes, there was definitely a problem—with him. But how to tell him? She chewed on her bottom lip. Mentally she shrugged. Might as well try his tactic and just blurt it out. "It was your sermon—or rather, the way you delivered your sermon."

His brows shot upward. "I'm sorry if you didn't like the subject—"

She shook her head. "It wasn't that—"

"I chose it especially for you—"

He had wanted a reason for her leaving the church, and she would give it to him. "I left yesterday because I was angry."

"With whom?" He appeared surprised.

"You."

He frowned, his brows furrowing together. "What did I do?"

"Ya hoodwinked me into thinkin' ya were an excitin' and stimulatin' preacher. Ya made me think ya were differ'nt than my father—that ya were more carin' and understandin' of your parishioners' needs." There. She had said it. And she had to admit it felt good to get back at him. She held his stare.

He looked so shocked—so confused—so hurt.

Her triumph plummeted. It did not feel nearly as good as she had imagined it would. She had wanted to tell Aaron Gallagher this same thing for so long, but she had not had the courage. So, instead, once she had met Joshua and discovered that he, too, was like her father, she had immediately turned her anger onto him. So where was the satisfaction she had hoped to obtain?

Joshua's eyes dimmed. His nostrils flared ever so slightly with his intake of breath. He was angry.

She could see it in his expression. Pain and anger, and both directed at her. *Well, now you've gone and done it, DeeDee. I hope you're proud of yourself.* But she did not feel very pleased at all—more like ashamed, even remorseful.

"Anything else?"

Hearing the slow burn smoldering in his voice, she trembled. "I—uh—" Geez. Now how was she going to fix things? *You always do this, DeeDee. Ya ask for trouble—ya make people upset, then when ya do, ya can't ever figure out how they got that way.* She held herself rigid. Well, she certainly knew how *this* had happened, did she not? "Look, Josh, I didn't mean it like that."

"It's *Joshua*, and just exactly how did you mean it? I think you were pretty clear." He glared at the river, then stabbed her with a scowl. "Somehow or another you feel that I've compromised my parishioners, and that I'm not fulfilling my job to the best of my abilities. Oh, no, DeeDee, I think you've made yourself abundantly clear."

"Now, hold on just a minute." DeeDee's temper met his head on. "I don't deserve all this. Ya did ask me what was wrong yesterday. Did ya want me to *lie* to ya?"

He stared at her for a second. His posture slumped a little. "No."

The simple reply pierced her like an arrow.

"That's the trouble." He peered down at the ground. "What you said is true."

DeeDee swallowed. Did she dare venture further? "If you know that, Joshua—" She paused, uncertain if she should continue. She softened her voice. "Why don't ya preach the way ya did out there in the meadow the other day?"

Eyes trained on the space of earth between them, he did not answer.

"Oh, Josh—ua." Her mouth suddenly went dry. She had no right to be telling this man how to run his business with the Lord, but since he obviously did not know, somebody had to do it. Apparently, he had not gotten the message himself. "You were so good."

His head still held at a downward tilt, he peered up at her.

"I've never heard such a powerful talk. And the children—" Rearing back a little, she smiled approvingly. "They were captivated by your tale."

He cocked his head to one side, the twinkle in his eyes growing a little brighter.

"That story—"

"About the Catholics and the Protestants?" He suddenly appeared more interested.

She nodded with a smile. "It was so—so enlightening—so uplifting." She gestured toward him with a fist. "You had all of us completely involved. Ya described everythin' so well that it was easy to absorb your meanin'. I've never enjoyed a sermon as much as I did that one."

Joshua raised up straight, and a full sparkle of appreciation lighted his eyes.

She watched his demeanor shift from anger and frustration to an encouraged expression of pride and accomplishment. "Really, Joshua." She rushed on with the moment. If praise was what was needed to stimulate his effort, then praise was what she would give him. "I thoroughly enjoyed your sermon in the meadow." Feeling the strength of his perusal, she lowered her voice to a mere whisper. "It was wonderful. You should've never changed it."

He watched her another moment before looking at the river. He inhaled slowly. "I'd like to preach like that all the time," he said despondently.

"Then why don't ya?"

Staring off with a faraway gaze, he shook his head. "The people of Harmony aren't ready for anything like that."

DeeDee frowned. What was he talking about?

"You see how things are around here," he said defensively. He looked back at her. "Folks are used to the old ways of preaching. Why, they can't even tolerate a simple thing like someone dressing differently, or talking differently."

DeeDee tensed. She knew he meant her. Wanting to show her indifference, she shrugged. "So what? Eventually they'll get used to it."

"But I don't want them to get used to it," he all but shouted.

DeeDee flinched. What had made him so angry again?

Obviously seeing her distress, he relaxed his posture as well as his tone. "I want them to be like you say you were. I want them to enjoy it. I want them to learn from it and, hopefully, to apply it to their lives."

"But don't ya see?" DeeDee shifted, leaning a little nearer. "That's exactly what'll happen."

He squinted at her as if he did not believe what she said.

"Look, Joshua. If ya deliver God's word with the same feelin', the same passion as ya did the other mornin' in the meadow"—she waved her hand in the direction of the church—"those folks in Harmony're goin' to be fallin' all over themselves tryin' to hear every word ye've got to tell 'em." She hesitated a moment, waiting for his reaction.

He did not speak. He just kept staring at her, his expression one of amazement.

"Joshua, can't ya see the gift ya have? Ye've got more potential to influence these people's lives than I've ever bore witness to." She shook her head. The man was utterly unbelievable. It was only too apparent that he was completely unaware of his own strength of character.

Plucking a blade of grass from the ground, she ripped it down the center, then tossed it to one side. "I just don't understand. Why can't you see it?" she said under her breath. Shifting her attention to the river, she sighed disheartedly. If only she could make him see—make him understand his own self-worth and power.

Her mind tortured her further. *Oh, yeah, DeeDee, you're a great one to be giving advice. The only thing you've ever accomplished in your life is total anarchy. You're nothin' more than a rebel without a revolution.*

"How is it you know so much about things like . . . like passion?"

Joshua's voice was so soft, so cautious-sounding, that DeeDee was not certain she had actually heard him speak. She darted him a inquisitive glance. "Excuse me?"

He smiled shyly. "I said, how is it you know so much about something like passion?"

"I'm not sure I follow ya." That was a lie—at least partly. Looking at him, she saw the return of that strange glimmer she had observed in his eyes when she had fallen on top of him.

His pupils appeared larger than she had ever seen.

Her heart thudded in her chest. Her earlier nervousness returned. She might not know *exactly* what he meant, but she at least had a pretty good idea of what he was leading up to, and it both thrilled and frightened her.

"I wish I had your confidence. I wish I could be more like you, and not worry so much about what others think of me. I wish . . ." He leaned toward her, his gaze filled with desire.

DeeDee swallowed. Oh, Lord. Here it was. He was finally going to kiss her. What was she supposed to do? Her nerves raced up and down her body. She could not think. He was so close now, only a breath separated them. "What do you wish, Joshua?" she whispered with a struggling gasp.

"I wish . . ." His mouth touched hers. He pulled back a space and looked at her.

Shivers rippled through DeeDee from the inside out.

"I wish you wouldn't talk anymore . . ." He slipped a hand up to the back of her head and pulled her to him.

Willingly, yet fearfully, she met his kiss.

Light and warm, his lips brushed hers.

The tiny pinpricks of his late-evening chin stubble teased her skin. She flinched, but did not pull away. His mouth felt slightly scratchy and foreign, yet oh-so-wondrous against the softness of hers. Her head swam within a frenzy of emotions. Her body heated, igniting into a fevered flame.

Timidly at first, he slid his tongue over the part between her lips.

Uncertain of what to do, she did not resist.

He pressed her farther, delving his tongue into the recesses of her mouth.

From somewhere deep in her throat, she moaned. Her senses became alive, electrifying her flesh. She eased a hand up to his chest, half-touching his shirt, half-caressing his bare skin, wholly inflaming her.

Moving closer still, he clasped a hand around her waist, the urgency in his touch only too apparent. Like a man possessed, he groaned, bruising her lips with his sudden fierceness.

DeeDee answered his strained moan with a tortured whimper. She did not think about the wrong or right of it—she did not want to. For if she allowed a single thought of doubt to enter her brain, the moment might be lost forever. She clutched the fabric of his shirt, wadding it in her fist, then hooked her other hand around his neck, digging her nails into his skin.

He groaned, sure pain echoing in the sound.

His sunburn. Oh, God. She wrenched her mouth from his and released her grip. She had forgotten about the sunburn. "I'm sorry," she whispered, more than a little out of breath.

Shaking his head, he smiled. "It's all right." He pulled away, sliding his hands down the length of her arms, to her wrists. "It's just as well."

DeeDee frowned. What did he mean by that? Was he sorry he had kissed her? It was true, this was her first kiss, but was it really

all that bad for him? It certainly was not
for her.

He looked up at the sky. "We should probably
go back to the boardinghouse. As it is, we're only
going to get a few hours of sleep."

What *had* she done? Why had he suddenly turned
cold? "What's wrong, Joshua?" she asked hesitantly, not knowing if she truly wanted to hear the
answer.

Taking in a deep breath, he shook his head again.
"Nothing."

DeeDee narrowed a look of disbelief on him.

He chuckled. "All right, actually there is. But I
won't be able to talk to you about it if I don't—"
Suddenly appearing shy, he looked away, then
gazed at her again. "There is something I need
to discuss with you—something of great impor-
tance."

DeeDee shivered. Oh, no. This could not be
happening. It was too soon—too quick. Geez, he
had only just now kissed her for the first time.
Surely he did not mean to speak of marriage at
this early date? Maybe *he* was in a hurry to take
a wife, but she was not yet ready for a husband.
"Uh—Joshua, yer right. We should get back to the
boardinghouse."

He nodded. "In a minute. I want to—"

"No, really, yer right." Jumping to her feet, she
gathered her bath toiletries as quickly as she could.
"It *is* late, and I *am* tired." She faked a yawn that
soared into a real one.

"Wait, DeeDee, this is important."

But she was not about to wait around and listen. This was all happening too fast. It *was* possible that she might be falling in love with Joshua Wylie, but she could not think about that right now. It was still too soon, and she was still too new to all of these emotions he had inflamed within her.

"No, DeeDee, listen to what I have to tell—"

Without further hesitation, she backed a few steps in the direction of town. She shook her head. "I'm sleepin' in late tomorrow, and I promised to take Lizzy and Joey swimmin' in the afternoon, so—"

She wheeled away, heading for the boarding-house as fast as she could move without hopefully revealing her true anxiety. "I'll talk to ya tomorrow after supper, okay? 'Night," she called with a backward wave.

Then, training her sights on the church steeple gleaming in the moonlight, she dashed for the safety of her room. Feeling enormously giddy, yet greatly relieved, when she finally reached the front door of the boardinghouse, she smiled up at the paint job she had accomplished on Zeke's shop. "And to think, DeeDee . . ." She ran her fingertips over her lips, remembering the excitement of Joshua's kiss. "Tonight never would've taken place, if it weren't for a few speckles of yellow paint."

# ♥ Chapter 10

JOSHUA AWOKE THE next day to Miss Minnie's insistent, high-pitched rendition of "Beautiful Dreamer." He peeked out from beneath the pillow covering his face and squinted at the light beaming in through the window. He groaned. After having to suffer through such a sleepless night with his back, no matter how late in the day it might be now, it was still entirely too early to have to endure such sound.

"Beautiful Dreamer, wake unto me. Starlight and moonbeams are waiting for thee. . . ."

Glorious Lord. Had the woman no pity? What he would not give for the usual morning disturbance of a robin's warble, or the twitter of a sparrow. Even the screeching caw of a crow would be more preferable. Turning from his side to his stomach, he yanked the pillow more securely atop his head, but it did not help.

Frustrated, and in pain from his sunburn, he tossed the coverlets away, then sat up. Draping his legs over the side of the mattress, he leaned down and rested his elbows on his knees, then rubbed his face. What a cruel night he had experienced. Very little sleep, the torturous stinging of his back, disconnected thoughts of DeeDee, and now Miss Minnie's singing.

He sucked in a replenishing breath, then straightened, groaning against the nettling bites nipping at his skin. He had been unable to bear wearing anything on his back, so he had opted to sleep shirtless, though it had not helped much. Moving slowly, he stretched his muscles. It irked him to think of having to bother the doctor with something as trivial as a sunburn, but maybe DeeDee had been right. Maybe it was bad enough to have it checked.

Rising, he walked to the wardrobe closet and opened one of the doors. He turned his back toward the mirror, then looked over his shoulder. He shot his reflection an anguished scowl. Except for the white X crisscrossing his skin, from his neck to the top edge of his long underwear, his back glared red with various-sized water blisters.

When he had looked at it last night in the lamp's glow, it had not appeared so fiery. Now, in the daylight, it was only too clear just how bad it truly was. Releasing a dispirited and weary sigh, he shook his head. How could he have been so preoccupied so as not to have noticed the heat the previous afternoon when he was working?

He moved for his clothing. Gingerly he stepped into a pair of Levi's, then retrieved another of his worn, yet soft workshirts from the wardrobe. He could not stand the thought of wearing the rough and starchy suit of the clergy, not now.

Once he had dressed, he quietly left his room, escaping the aggravation of Miss Minnie's singing only after he had departed the boardinghouse. Bright yellow, Zeke's barbershop snatched his attention.

DeeDee. The previous night's conversation with her by the river filtered into his brain along with another round of the older woman's serenade. Yes, how could he have been so preoccupied, indeed? There was only one answer—DeeDee. He closed the door behind him, then headed for the doctor's office.

DeeDee Gallagher was certainly starting to be quite a persistent subject in his life. No matter what he did, or where he went, she always seemed to pop up in his daily endeavors. And even if she, herself, was not present, it seemed someone was always talking about her. Talking about her. The phrase triggered the subject he had wanted to discuss with her last night.

He peered around in search of her. She had to be informed of what had gone on at the meeting of the Ladies' Auxiliary meeting. After he visited the doctor, he would most assuredly see to that *talk* he had tried to have with her the previous night. Passing the office of the *Sentinel,* Joshua looked inside.

Billy Taylor stood leaning over a desk study-ing a stack of papers. Seeing Joshua, he visibly blanched. "Reverend Wylie," he said, his voice echoing through the building with a nervous inflection.

Joshua smiled, then motioned for him to come outside.

"Yessir, Reverend, can I help ya with somethin'?" The boy swallowed hard.

Joshua nodded toward the office. "Is that the latest edition of 'Under the Shell'?"

Darting a wary glance in the direction of the papers still lying on the desk, Billy looked back at Joshua and nodded. "I was jist about to take 'em out."

"May I see one?" Normally, Joshua did not uphold the reading of Billy's gossip column, but today it might be nice to have a little distraction from his back.

Billy's brows shot up. "Ya wanna see it?"

"Sure, why not?" After fishing in his pocket for some change, Joshua pulled out a penny.

"But—I, um—I didn't think ya liked that sorta thing."

"Well, not usually." What was wrong with the kid? Did he not want to sell a paper? "But I thought you might have written something about how much you enjoyed DeeDee Gallagher's teach-ing on Sunday."

The boy froze. "Ya know about that?"

Joshua nodded. "It was my idea."

Billy's Adam's apple bobbed. "Oh," he said simply.

"Can I buy one now?" Joshua asked, leaning into the kid's line of vision.

"Um—yeah—just a minute." With that, he dashed inside, gathered the sheaves, then darted back out. "Here ya go," he hollered, shoving the paper into Joshua's hand. Then, spinning around, he tore down the street at a full run.

Joshua held up the penny. "Hey, what about your money?"

Billy did not pay him any attention. He did not even so much as acknowledge the question.

"What's gotten into him?" Joshua said to himself as he scanned the headlines.

UNDER THE SHELL

*JUDGING DELILAH*

by Billy Taylor

Instantly Joshua felt the hairs on the back of his neck stand at attention.

> Newest town arrival, Miss Delilah Gallagher, has definitely given our town a new wake-up call. Only minutes after her train pulled in, she near drowned the minister. Then, after telling the most gall-derned, uproarious, and indisputably exciting Sunday school lesson

this reporter has ever attended, she decides
to change the entire color scheme of the town,
starting off with her own Uncle Zeke Gallgher's
barbershop. And in case you haven't seen it yet,
it's that bright good-morning-yellow building
between the boardinghouse and the jail.

Joshua tensed. He glared after Billy. Did he have
to mention all the antics that had occured since
DeeDee had come to town? He continued to read.

Needless to say, the Ladies' Auxiliary is
none too happy with her choice, not to mention Miss Gallagher's decision to change the
town's color scheme without their permission.
Too bad. Maybe they need to re-think their
thinking. Maybe it is just what was needed to
brighten up the town, in addition to her colorful dress and talk. Yes, Delilah Gallagher sure
has given us a new wake-up call. The question
unnerving the Auxiliary now is, what's she
gonna serve up for breakfast?

Joshua couldn't believe it. After crumpling the
paper, he stuffed it into his pants pocket. It
was nice of Billy to try to defend her, but why
did it all have to be brought up again, and in
print?

He was just now getting to know DeeDee, but
not yet as personally and intimately as he would
like. He was not fully certain why, but he wanted
that opportunity. If only the townsfolk could see
beyond her appearance and give her a chance, who
knew what would happen? They just might grow
to like each other.

The sound of children's laughter rippled up from somewhere near the river.

He looked in that direction. Hadn't DeeDee said something last night about taking the Tolliver kids for a swim? Facing the treeline edging the water, he searched the area for any sign of her. He could not see her. He strained his hearing.

Another vault of laughter echoed over the businesses of the town.

He would have to find her and talk to her right away. This could not wait—not even until supper. He could not—would not let this happen. Having his sunburn tended was going to have to be put off until later. He was going to have to put an end to this, and now.

The closer he came to the water, the louder the children's play grew. Nearing the mill, he finally saw her.

Pantlegs rolled up to her knees, DeeDee stood in the water, laughing and splashing with Lizzy and Joey Tolliver.

Good. After cutting a look around the area to make sure no one else was present, he marched up to the edge of the riverbank. "DeeDee?"

Obviously startled, she whipped around. She appeared even more surprised to see him. "Joshua." She smiled sweetly, then shot a furtive glance at the children. "How's yer back?" she asked, wading a few steps toward him.

"DeeDee, I need to talk to you."

She stopped a couple of feet away from him, her pleased expression turning a little fearful. She lowered her voice. "I thought we decided to talk tonight—after supper."

"No, *you* decided that," he stated firmly. "I didn't agree to anything."

She looked back at the kids swimming toward her. "Can't it wait? I'm kinda busy right now."

"No, it can't." He was not about to be thwarted this time. "It's urgent that we speak now."

"C'mon, DeeDee!" Joey yelled, then tossed up a handful of water.

Some of it splashed in Joshua's face. It did not serve to cool the growing tension rising in him. He could see he was not going to be able to talk to her here. He was going to have to get her away from the children. "I need to talk to you now, DeeDee."

"Joshua, I really think—"

"I don't care what you think, I need to talk to you right now." He grabbed her hand, then pulled her toward the bank.

"Joshua!" She tried to yank out of his grasp, but he held on tight. She glared at him, then cut the kids a nervous look, before returning her attention to him.

"Look, DeeDee, this is important, or I wouldn't be insistent."

She peered deeper at him, her expression puzzled. "Look, I'm busy. I just don't have the time to sit and chat right now, so if you'll just please do like I asked and wait till later?"

"No." He took a minute to gather his thoughts. It would not have been easy to try and explain her predicament under the best of circumstances. "You need to be told this now."

With forceful movements she eased out of his grasp, her eyes daring him to make a scene. "Not in front of the children."

"I agree," he said, searching for somewhere more private.

"Wh-what's wr-wrong, DeeDee?" Lizzy inquired once she had paddled into shallow waters. Brows knitted, she shot an inquisitive glance between Joshua and DeeDee. "Are y-y-you two ma-mad at e-e-each other?"

"No, honey," DeeDee answered, then scooped up the child.

Joshua also assured Lizzy with a shake of his head. "I just need to talk to DeeDee for a few minutes. Do you think you and your brother can play here on the sandbank for a little bit?" Taking the child out of the woman's arms, he returned her to the water.

Lizzy looked at DeeDee. "You s-s-sure you're no-not ma-mad at e-e-each other?"

Arching a brow, DeeDee peered at Joshua, then smiled back at the little girl. "No. Reverend Wylie's not mad."

Joshua almost grinned in spite of his mood. She had said *he* was not, but was *she*? He searched what he was certain was a forced expression of nonchalance. Oh, yes. DeeDee Gallagher was definitely upset, but not nearly as angry as he knew she would be by the time he finished telling her what he had come to talk about.

Once she had instructed both kids to remain in the shallows, DeeDee waded out of the water with him.

"How about behind the mill?" Joshua asked, pointing to a clump of bushes at the rear of the building.

DeeDee shot one last glance at the children.

"They'll be fine. We're close enough that you can hear them if there's a problem." Without waiting for any further objections, Joshua took her elbow and gently, but firmly, led her toward the designated spot.

His shoes squeaked a squishy protest. He cringed inwardly. *Not now, Lord, please.*

DeeDee chuckled. "Ya know, I've noticed ya have a slight water problem with yer shoes."

Grimacing, Joshua held his temper in check. He had been so determined to make DeeDee see the urgency of their talk, he had not noticed that he had walked into the river up to his ankles. "Only when certain young ladies are around." He had not meant to sound so accusing, but now was not the time to be humorous.

Almost immediately after they had reached the corner of the building, DeeDee pulled out of his grasp. "Okay, *Mister* Wylie, what's so important that it just can't wait until tonight?"

"Look, DeeDee." He paused. He was not looking forward to any of this. "There's no easy way to break this to you, so—"

"Joshua." She held up a hand. "I think I know what this's about, and—"

"You do?" How could that be? She had been painting when the Ladies' Auxiliary had met.

She nodded, looked away a second, then gifted him with a shy smile. "I have to tell ya, inasmuch as I like ya and all, I don't think I'm quite ready for this."

"Ready for what?" It did not matter whether or not *she* was ready; Lillie Taylor had already made up her mind. And where Lillie went, others followed. "DeeDee, I think you should just listen to me."

Taking a deep breath, she squared her shoulders. "Okay, but just remember, I tried to warn ya."

Joshua stared at her. She was not making any sense. He forced her comment aside. Now there were more pressing issues to discuss. "It seems we've got a little problem," he started off, but did not know how or where to go from there.

"What d'ya mean, problem?" Her body went rigid.

Joshua took a deep breath, then retrieved the wadded paper out of his pocket. "Here. I think you'd better read this." Handing the wrinkled gossip column to her, he squared his shoulders, preparing for the worst. He hated to tell her this way, but he did not know how else to go about it. He had not had much experience in breaking this kind of news to someone. He watched her face as she read.

Her cheeks flamed bright scarlet. Her breathing quickened, and her bottom lip trembled.

In the background he heard the children splashing each other. He checked to make sure they were where they were supposed to be. Assured that they had only moved a little closer to the mill, he looked back at DeeDee.

"What is this?" she asked, her voice angry.

"It's called the 'Under the—' "

"I can see that much for myself, but what exactly is it?"

"It's a gossip column that Billy Taylor writes for the Harmony *Sentinel.*"

"Billy Taylor?" she asked, surprise marking her tone. "I thought after Sunday he had maybe started to like me."

"He does; he did defend you a bit."

"Oh, yeah. I can sure see that. Then why did he have to mention all those things?" She stared down at the print, tears forming in her eyes. Wheeling away from him, she covered her mouth with her hand.

He could see by the quiver of her shoulders that she had started to cry. "I'm sorry, DeeDee," he said, stepping up behind her. "I don't understand why everybody's in such an uproar about you. I think your antics are cute."

"Cute!" She spun back on him. With red-rimmed eyes, she glared at him, jamming the paper into his chest. "You think all of this's just some kind of prank on my part for—for attention'r somethin', don't ya?"

Surprised by her sudden change in temperament, he flinched. "It doesn't matter what I think."

"Oh, yes, it does," she said heatedly. "Geez." She waved her hands, emphasizing her rage. "You and this whole town're not about to give me a chance, are ya? Ya all had yer mind made up about me the minute ya heard my name."

"Now, wait just a—"

"I know what ya think. I know what everybody thinks. Delilah, forget the Gallagher part. The name, Delilah, had all of ya hooked into that nasty Bible stuff right from the start. I guess it just *goes* with the name, huh? It doesn't matter that I'm not anythin' like Sampson's Delilah. None of ya care."

"Do you?" Joshua's temper edged closer to the surface. Surely she had to agree that she was at least partly to blame for how everyone felt about her.

She stared at him, disbelief registering in her expression. "What's that supposed to mean? Of course *I* care. It's me we're talkin' about, isn't it?"

Joshua nodded. There was no easy way out of this now. He might as well bring everything out into the open. "Look, I know knocking me into the trough was just a simple accident—"

"So ya *do* think like everybody else?"

"Now, *you* hold on a minute." He pointed a finger at her, demanding her silence. "I've listened to what you had to say—now you listen to me."

Clasping her hands in front of her, DeeDee pursed her lips and scowled, and though her eyes emitted a challenge, she remained quiet.

"You have to have known something like this was bound to happen."

She opened her mouth to speak, but he thwarted her efforts with another punctuation of his finger.

"Hear me out. I've been witness to just about everything you've done around town."

"Like what—painting Uncle Zeke's shop?"

Joshua sighed. It was only too apparent that he was going to have to talk fast if he intended on making his point before she butted in again. "That, and everything else. However humorous it might have been, *you* knew it would cause a scene, didn't you?"

This time she did not speak. She only looked at him and blinked like some great-horned owl in a tree.

"And that Bible lesson—" He wanted to smile, but kept it in check. He shook his head. "Injuns, DeeDee? That was very creative."

She shrugged. "They listened, didn't they? The way I heard it, it was the first time they've ever truly enjoyed one of their lessons." She tipped her head to one side, then narrowed an inquisitive stare on him. "Besides, how'd ya know it was Injuns? One of the kids tell ya?"

He waved a dismissing hand at her. "Don't change the subject." Lord, no. He could not let her shift the focus onto him. If she did, he might have to admit his Sunday morning indiscretion. "And what about that paint? Why bright yellow of all colors? You had to know it was going to upset the Ladies' Auxiliary."

"Look," she interrupted, her eyes stabbing him like shards of frosty glass. "Those *ladies*, as you put it, don't have anythin' to do with my paintin' Uncle Zeke's shop. He hated that icky ol' green. He even said so himself. And as for why I did it—it's because he did somethin' nice for me. I just returned the favor by paintin' his shop with his favorite color. He said he liked it. Said that'd been the color he'd have chosen if he'd been given the option."

She shot a glare toward town, her tears returning. "But, of course, that doesn't matter, does it?" Her anger resurfaced. "All everybody sees is that hussy, Delilah, messin' up their perfect little town." She waved her hands despondently and started to walk away. "Well, they can have it! I'm not waitin' for summer."

"DeeDee," Joshua called after her. Catching up to her after only a few steps, he spun her back to face him. "What do you mean by that?"

"I *mean*—" She leaned forward and glowered at him. "I'm leavin'. Uncle Zeke wanted me to stay for the first part of the summer and help him with the shop so's I could earn money to get out to San Francisco like I want." She took a breath. "But now—now I'm just so blamed mad I could swallow a horned toad backward."

Joshua had to clear his throat to keep from laughing at that one.

Even so, she must have seen his strain, and was not amused. "Ya think it's funny? Ya think *I'm* funny? Good!" She nearly spat the word at him. "Then you'll be even happier to find out ya can definitely count me outta yer little courtin' game.

And ya can also count me gone for San Francisco."
She spun away from him again, then stomped off
toward town.

Courtin' game? Where had *that* come from, and
what did it mean? And what was all this business
about going to San Francisco? This was the first he
had heard of her leaving. "DeeDee, please, you're
not really going to let this town beat you, are you?"
He hurried after her. "Come on, now, let's try to
figure out what to do rationally."

"Rationally? Geez. When did anythin' dealin'
with *rational* come into play here? Don't ya know
anythin' about us *Delilahs*?" Stopping, she set her
hands on her hips, then started to pace in front of
him, seething fury etching her features whenever
she looked at him. "Delilahs are hussies! They're
hell-bent on causin' nothin' but problems for every
Tom, Sampson, and oh, yeah, Joshua of the whole
human race."

She flicked her wrist back at the spot where the
gossip page lay on the ground. "Read it for yerself.
It's all right there in black and white. They're
just not going to get used to me and leave me
alone." Halting, she leaned into his face. "Even
the kids think I'm strange—just ask Billy Taylor.
He'll tell ya."

Joshua shook his head. His heart went out to her.
Lord, how he hated to see her in so much pain. And
she was. He could see it in the tears escaping her
temper. He tried to wipe one away. "DeeDee—"

"Don't," she said, knocking his hand away. She
swiped away the tear herself, then sucked in a

shuddering breath. "Ya don't have to coddle me. I can take care of myself."

"Who said anything about coddling you?" Hesitantly he brushed aside a stray strand of her auburn hair.

This time she did not try to stop him. She looked so pitiful, so alone, and so hurt.

He wanted to grab her and hold her close, but he did not dare. He was not sure how she would react. At this moment she did not appear very receptive to his trying to comfort her. What was he to do? How could he approach her with any kind of help when he, himself, had no idea how to go about it? He slipped his hand down her arm and twined his fingers with hers. "Why don't we take a few minutes to just sit down and—"

A loud shrill of a scream attacked his hearing.

Oh, Lord. The children. He had momentarily forgotten about them. Instantly he looked up in the direction where they had left them playing.

They were nowhere to be seen.

"I don't see them." Dread lodging in his throat, Joshua looked at DeeDee.

"Oh, God, no," she murmured, her gaze locking with his. Her face drained of color. Then, wheeling away, she sped around the side of the mill.

Somewhere in the back of his brain, panic triggered his memory. A short while earlier he had vaguely remembered hearing the sound of the paddle wheel begin to whirl through the water. But he had been so caught up in his argument with DeeDee, he had not paid it any attention.

"DeeDee!" Joey screamed.

"Lord in heaven." Joshua did not wait for further prodding. The children were in trouble. He ran around the other side of the mill and burst in the huge front door. "Stop the wheel! Stop the wheel!"

The men working inside just stared at him. No one moved.

DeeDee cried out for him.

A child shrieked again.

Joshua's heart slammed against his chest. Its pounding echoed in his brain. "For pity's sake, men!" Unable to voice his fear, he looked around. He had no idea how a gristmill worked. How was he going to stop the paddle from spinning? "We have to stop the wheel," he said, pointing out the huge window. "One of the children may be hurt."

Immediately a man ran to a huge lever and shoved it up.

In the background the loud churning of water slowly came to a dead silence.

"Joshua!" DeeDee yelled again, her voice edging on torment.

He dashed out and around to the side of the huge mill.

He could not see either of the children. But hanging on to one of the large spokes, standing on another, DeeDee leaned down to the enormous hub at the center of the wheel. Soaking wet, her back toward him, she looked over her shoulder at Joshua. "Get the doctor!" she shouted.

"Lizzy's hurt. Her head's bleedin' bad, and her arm's caught."

"Get the doctor," Joshua repeated the command to one of the men that had joined him from inside. Then, without waiting, he rushed headlong into the water. Half-wading, half-swimming, he raced to the paddle. Grabbing hold, he started to pull himself up.

"Careful!" DeeDee shouted tearfully. "If you upset the paddle, it might tear her arm off." She was crying hard now.

"Hold on to her," Joshua instructed. "I'll be right there."

"Lizzy—Lizzy," Joey wailed as he bobbed beside the huge disk. He looked at Joshua. "It's my fault. I made her do it."

"Go to the bank, Joey," Joshua ordered.

The boy shook his head. "It's my fault—it's my fault." The kid was crying so hard he could hardly keep his head above water.

Joshua scowled back at the group of men gathering at the edge of the river. "One of you." He had to get Joey away from the wheel. "Get the boy."

Immediately three men jumped into the river.

Then, with careful movements, Joshua climbed the large spokes until he had worked his way over to DeeDee. Gripping the wood frame, he stepped around her to the other side.

Her sobs clutched his heart. He peered down at the lifeless child, wedged into the hub by one frail little arm. Terror filled his soul. Fear lanced his determination.

"We've got to get her down from here," DeeDee insisted, reaching inside the center of the wheel.

"Wait," Joshua instructed. "If we move her, we could do more harm than good. Let's see how bad it is." He looked down, examining the child.

Blood smeared the entire left side of her face, dripping down from her temple to her neck. Her arm looked as if it were nearly wrenched from its socket, and her eyes were closed. She did not appear to be breathing, and—

With a wordless prayer on his lips, he leaned down and listened against the little girl's back. He swallowed hard, and looked up at DeeDee's fearful expression. His soul mirrored her agony. Against the flowing current beneath them, he could not hear a heartbeat.

# ♥ Chapter 11
♥

ARMS HELD TIGHTLY across her middle, DeeDee leaned against the far porch support beam outside the Tolliver house. She stared down at the clean-swept planks, her mind whirling with emotion.

How had she let this happen? How could she have been so thoughtless as to leave the children alone on the riverbank? She knew how determined Joey had always been to play on the paddle wheel like the older children. And, of course, it only served to follow that Lizzy would want to do the same as her older brother.

Once again DeeDee's eyes overflowed with tears as she envisioned Lizzy's tiny form lying so still and lifeless in Mrs. Tolliver's large bed. *God in heaven*, she prayed harder than she had ever prayed in her life. *Please don't let that child die.*

The doctor had said that Lizzy's shoulder was only dislocated, and though she had been forced to swallow a great deal of water, he had assured all that she was most definitely alive. However, the bump she had received on her temple was a different matter all together. She had not, as yet, regained consciousness.

He could not say for certain whether or not the girl ever would. The next twenty-four hours were critical. "Where medicine is concerned, the brain is an uncertainty," he had reported after treating her other injuries. "We know so little as to how it works, and even less about how it heals itself."

The longer Lizzy remained in what the doc had called a *coma*, the worse the prognosis.

And it was all DeeDee's fault. She couldn't meet the eyes of anyone in town.

Lillie Taylor sat on the large swing with a grief-stricken Nancy Tolliver huddled next to her. Billy stood close to his mother.

"She looks so pitiful with her tear-stained eyes," Maisie whispered, looking at DeeDee. Feet planted firmly on the planked floor, she sat in a spindle-chair next to Minnie, a handkerchief twisted in her fingers.

Minnie, with the ever-close-by Ruth Alice beside her, seesawed in a rocker directly across from the anguished woman.

"It's true, Miss Minnie. But she should know better than to have ever let Lizzie out of her sight," Ruth Alice stated.

All eyes turned DeeDee's way.

A nervous quiver raced up her spine, but she did not waver from her post. She was determined to wait out Lizzy's unconsciousness. Gripping tightly to her inner strength, she remained at a discreet distance from the others, but would not give up her vigilance.

"I heard she was lollygagging over behind the mill with the Reverend," Billy piped in.

"Billy Taylor!" Maisie said in a hiss. "Hush now."

DeeDee bristled. What exactly did he mean by *lollygagging?* She chanced a peek up.

"You'd think after all the strife that she's caused poor Nancy, here, she'd at least have the decency to leave," Lillie grumbled, though it was plain to DeeDee the woman had meant for her to hear it.

No longer inflicted with red eyes, Rebecca Ellen Russell sat poised pretty as a newly blossomed sunflower. "Remember what Jesus tells us in the New Testament, Matthew seven thirteen and fourteen, Miss Maisie. 'Enter ye in at the strait gate: for wide is the gate, and broad is the way, that leadeth to destruction, and may there be which go in thereat: Because strait is the gate, and narrow is the way, which leadeth unto life, and few there be that find it.' "

Cringing inwardly, DeeDee squeezed her eyes closed with a shudder. Even Rebecca, with her constant touting of Bible verses, thought DeeDee had done wrongly.

Footsteps approached.

"And—" The angry tone of Joshua's voice stabbed through the women's discord.

DeeDee flinched.

As one, except for Nancy Tolliver, the ladies snapped their attentions to him.

Now changed into his customary black suit and clerical collar, he stepped onto the porch.

Zeke sauntered up behind him.

"If you were to continue reading in Matthew seven seventeen through twenty," Joshua said, picking up where he had left off, "you would see where Jesus also states, 'Even so every good tree bringeth forth good fruit; but a corrupt tree bringeth forth evil fruit. A good tree cannot bring forth evil fruit, neither can a corrupt tree bring forth good fruit. Every tree that bringeth not forth good fruit is hewn down, and cast into the fire. Wherefore by their fruits ye shall know them." He pointed at DeeDee. "This woman has done nothing wrong. She's a good and God-fearing person."

Lillie Taylor pulled up straight, her expression filled with surprise. "Surely you're not suggesting—"

Zeke edged a step closer to DeeDee. Her bottom lip trembled uncontrollably. They were right. She should not be here.

"'Judge not, that ye be not judged. For with what judgment ye judge, ye shall be judged,' Lillie Taylor."

"Now, hold on, Reverend." Billy visibly stiffened. "That's my ma yer talkin' to."

"You stay out of this, boy," Joshua instructed.

DeeDee stared at him. She never seen him so angry, especially with anyone other than herself.

"I think you've done enough damage with that gossip column of yours. Why keep mentioning events that are over?"

"He was simply reporting the truth," Lillie interjected, taking hold of her son's hand.

DeeDee tried hard to stay in control of her emotions, but a sob escaped her throat.

"That's about enough!" Zeke's face turned red. "What harm has she done any a ya?" He glanced at Nancy. "Ya don't really hold my DeeDee responsible for what happened, do ya?"

"You stay out of this, too, Zeke Gallagher," Lillie demanded. "Of course you'd take her side. She's your niece."

"She's a helluva lot more than that—"

"I'll say she is," Lillie spouted in a huff. "It's been said that instead of watching Lizzy like she was *supposed* to be doing, she was trying to entice the reverend behind the mill."

"Stop it," DeeDee said, denying the remark with a shake of her head. It was one thing to fling such an accusation in her face when no one of consequence was around, but to do so in front of her uncle and Joshua—she shivered.

"You shut yer mouth, Lillie Taylor." Zeke held his hands loosely at his sides. He looked like he was a gunslinger waiting for the draw. "I'da never brought my girl out here from Pennsylvania if I'da thought she'da received *this* kinda treatment."

DeeDee's head buzzed with a whirlwind of emotions. *His* girl? What did Zeke mean by that?

"That wasn't how it happened at all," Joshua insisted. "*I* was the one who talked *her* into going behind the mill."

"You?" Zeke appeared instantly enraged. He glanced back at DeeDee. "What'd ya do to her?"

"Nothing." Looking at Zeke, Joshua took a step backward. "I wanted to talk to her—to tell her about how upset *these* fine women were over a new coat of paint and an interesting way of telling a Bible story."

DeeDee swallowed hard. She darted a sidelong glance at Joshua. And she had thought he had wanted to propose marriage. How could she have been so wrong? What a fool she had been to ever consider such a ludicrous notion.

"Stop it!" Nancy Tolliver lifted red-rimmed eyes to the faces standing before her.

DeeDee jumped.

Zeke stilled.

The others held to silence.

"How can you do this now?" Mrs. Tolliver's voice barely quavered above a whisper. Her eyes leveled on each face in turn. "My baby's lying in there fighting for her life, and all *you* can think about is persecuting this poor girl." She suddenly burst out in tears. "Go away—all of you. Take your judgments elsewhere. I'll not have you sully my home with them any longer."

DeeDee sucked in a breath. No one seemed to care how Lizzy's accident had affected Mrs. Tolliver or herself. They did not care that she was truly sorry for her neglectfulness of the children. Could they not see how she felt?

She had to get away from them all. Sobbing harder than she could remember crying in a very long time, she spun around and jumped down from the porch. Then, running with all her speed, she headed for the boardinghouse.

Catching sight of DeeDee, Joshua whipped around and started after her.

"No, Parson," Zeke called out.

Joshua halted mid-stride. "Somebody needs to go after her."

But before he could take so much as a single step, Zeke laid a hand on Joshua's forearm. "I'll go. It's my job."

"Don't you think it'll be better if I go?" Joshua persisted. "She doesn't appear to be to receptive right now. It might be better if *I* go to her. After all, I *am* her minister. She might listen to me better than anyone else."

Zeke sucked in a deep breath, his eyes taking on a faraway look. He shook his head. "No, Parson. I think it's 'bout time *I* talk to her. I got some purty important things to say to her." He sighed resolutely. "Some of 'em she ain't goin' to like . . . some of 'em I pray she does. Either way, though, it's high time she was told. I'm hopin' it'll make a difference in the way she feels 'bout lightin' out for San Francisco."

Joshua frowned. So she had told her uncle she was leaving, too. But what could DeeDee possibly need to know? And what difference could it make in her leaving or staying? "Don't you think she's already been through enough right now? She's pretty upset."

Zeke nodded, one eye squinting after his niece. "Madder'n a rained-on rooster."

Joshua bit down on the inside of his jaw to keep from smiling. No two people he had ever known before or since were quite as colorful in their descriptions as Zeke and DeeDee Gallagher. They were most definitely related.

"Still," Zeke continued, "she's got to be told some things. As it is, it's been too long waitin' now."

Watching the older man's expression, Joshua had a feeling that whatever the *something* was, it was going to be distasteful to Zeke, and even more upsetting for DeeDee. "You really think now's the wisest time to bring up your news, Zeke?"

"Nah, I don't." The whiskered man shook his head again, his eyes appearing almost tearful. "But then, neither has any other time in the last nineteen years." He started after her.

This time it was Joshua's turn to waylay Zeke. He grabbed the older man's upper arm. "Please, Zeke. Whatever troubles you, I'd ask you not to burden DeeDee with it just now. If it's truly as important as you've made it out to

be, I'm here. Talk to me. Let me help you
with it."

Zeke smiled, years of anguish dimming his usually bright eyes. He shrugged. "Ain't no help for
it, Parson." He shifted his sorrow-filled gaze in
the direction of DeeDee's departure. "And it's
'bout time I owned up to some things, and told
my girl, there, the truth." Then, without another word of explanation, he trudged toward the
boardinghouse.

Joshua glanced around at the women.

Billy hovering above them, they were all huddled
around Nancy, clucking and cooing about how sorry they were for intruding on her sorrow.

He returned his attention to Zeke's departure. He
was more worried about what the man had to say
to DeeDee. She did not need any more problems
thrust upon her right now, and by the way Zeke
had spoken, that was exactly what the older man
planned on doing.

Joshua stared after him, watching until Zeke had
moved out of sight. Maybe he should follow them
to the boardinghouse. He glanced back at the wom-
en on the porch. They did not seem to be going
anywhere too soon. He returned his attention to the
path leading to town. There would not be anyone
else at the boardinghouse except for DeeDee and
her uncle.

Maybe he *should* go, too, just in case. If this news
of Zeke's were devastating, she might need Joshua.
After all, he was the town minister. It was his duty
to aid a person in time of spiritual need. Convincing

himself that it was the only proper thing to do, he nodded, then proceeded to follow.

Once inside the boardinghouse, he searched out the interior until he heard DeeDee's voice echoing down from her room. Quietly he ascended the stairs, halting just outside her door.

It stood ajar a few inches.

He moved up closer. He could see DeeDee's reflection in the bureau mirror.

She was sitting on the foot of her bed. Her eyes were red, and she was still sobbing softly. "It's no good that you've come here, Uncle Zeke." She sniffled loudly. "I'm not goin' to let ya talk me outta goin' this time."

"That ain't why I'm here, girl, though after I'm finished tellin' ya what I gotta say, I hope ye'll change yer mind and stay for a while longer." He shrugged. "And if not . . . then I'll go with ya."

Joshua moved closer to the crack in the door. He was becoming most proficient in eavesdropping of late—especially where DeeDee was concerned. He shifted, trying to see the room clearly, but Zeke was nowhere in sight. The distance of the man's voice told Joshua he was relatively safe from being caught.

"That trick isn't goin' to work with me, Uncle Zeke. There's nothin' ya can do and nothin' ya can tell me that'll stop me this time." Standing abruptly, DeeDee squatted, then lunged back up and thumped a huge satchel down atop the bed. She strode to her wardrobe and flung open its doors. After gathering an armload of clothing, she returned to the bed and tossed it into the bag. "Nothin'!" she repeated in a determined tone.

"Hold on, girl. I mean what I say. If after I've said my piece, ya still wanna go to California, I *will* go with ya." One of Zeke's thick, trunklike arms moved into view. He grabbed DeeDee's hand. "Now, sit down and just hear me out."

"I don't want to listen." Covering her ears, DeeDee shook her head. "I've heard more than enough from the people in this town already."

"I ain't just *people*, girl—"

"Yeah, yer my uncle, and that's all." She snatched her arm out of his grasp, her pain-filled temper flashing in her eyes. "Ya can't stop me, ya know. It's not like yer my father or anythin'."

Zeke jumped fully into view. He grabbed DeeDee by the shoulders. "That's 'bout enough of yer peevishness, girl."

Joshua tensed. Surely the man did not intend on using force to make her listen to him, did he?

Zeke sucked in a deep breath, then released it with an audible sigh. "Look," he said, his voice suddenly softening. "This's goin' to be tough enough to say without havin' to put up with yer childish games."

"Games?" Apparently, DeeDee was determined to stand her ground. "I can assure ya, Uncle Zeke. This's not a game. I'm *goin'* to San Francisco, and that's final."

Still holding onto her, Zeke looked away for a minute. "How's 'bout we make another deal?"

"No." She held up her hands. "No deals—not again. I've had enough. Everybody in town hates me. They've had it in for me right from the start, and now I want *out*. No partnership, no 'I'm yer uncle and I want to get to know ya better'—nothin'. I just want to leave as quickly and as quietly as I can."

Joshua stiffened. Not that again. He could not deal with the thought of DeeDee leaving right now.

"And what 'bout Lizzy Tolliver?"

Joshua nodded and smiled with satisfaction. *Good man, Zeke.* It was obvious that the barber was determined to keep DeeDee in Harmony. Even if it meant he had to pull out the big guns against her.

DeeDee stilled. Her posture relaxed a bit. Then, slipping out of her uncle's grasp, she slumped down and sat on the edge of the bed.

Good. The little girl's name had hit its target.

Zeke moved across the room. He turned around, paused, and stared at her a moment, then began to pace across the short end of the room.

Joshua stepped away from the crack between the jamb and the door. He could not risk being caught before he learned what it was that Zeke felt necessary to tell DeeDee. He just couldn't bear for her to be hurt anymore.

"DeeDee, girl." The older man hesitated again. "What I got to say's goin' to come as a bit of a shock to ya."

DeeDee sniffled again.

Joshua leaned around and peeked inside again.

Positioned with his back to Joshua, Zeke held his hands clasped tightly behind him. "Ya know how ya was just tellin' me how I couldn't stop ya from leavin' on account of I'm just yer uncle?"

"I'm sorry, Uncle Zeke. I didn't mean to say that. I was just mad, and—"

He held up a hand, then resumed his pacing. Another pause.

Joshua swallowed. Never had he known Zeke to be at a loss for words.

He wiped the whiskers around his mouth as he would if he had just drunk a glass of milk. "Ya might of heard tell 'bout a gal I was sparkin' down El Paso way a long while back.'

DeeDee nodded, curiosity marking her tear-stained features.

"Well, sir, I might as well just blurt it out." Zeke sighed with a huff. "Her name was Callie Jean O'Day. And she was so purty—" An audible catch in his voice halted his words.

A lump formed in Joshua's throat as he continued to listen.

Zeke looked at DeeDee. His voice took on a soul-stirring tone as he continued. "Had hair 'bout the same color as yers, my Callie Jean did. Matter-a-factly, when I met her, she was just 'bout yer age, too."

"I don't understand. What's all this got to do with me?" DeeDee asked.

Joshua shot her a wary glance. The hairs on his arms rose. He shook his head slowly. He had a feeling he had a pretty good idea where this was all leading. *No, Lord, please don't let him tell her what I think he's going to say.*

"I'm gettin' to that part. Well." Zeke halted again and cleared his throat. "Like I said, we was sparkin'—planned on gettin' married, too."

"Uncle Zeke, that's sweet and very nice and all, but I still don't see where—"

He shot her an if-you'll-just-be-quiet-a-minute look, then continued. "Ya may not know this 'bout me, DeeDee, but in my younger days, I had a notable name for bein' fast with a gun. Matter-a-factly, until I met Callie Jean, that's how I made my livin'—wheelin' a gun, I mean."

"You really were a gunfighter, then?" DeeDee sounded in awe of his confession.

"Not 'zactly," Zeke answered. "I was a bounty hunter. But once I met up with yer—uh—with Callie Jean, that all changed. I swore to put them days behind me."

Fighting to ward off his feelings of suspicion, Joshua balled his hands into fists. Now he was positive he knew what was coming next.

"I overheard Mother and Father talkin' about the two of you one night," DeeDee informed her uncle. "They said a wanted man came gunnin' for ya, and the woman ran in front of you to protect you from a bullet."

Zeke nodded, his eyes glistening with tears. "She died then and there, in my arms." His voice quivered. He coughed, apparently for control, then continued. But this time his tone was harsh, angry.

"But not before I plugged that no-good-son-of-a-scorpion with a pill he couldn't digest."

Joshua stiffened. He had always known Zeke to be a hard man, but a fair one. Joshua felt certain Zeke was a soul in good standing with the Lord. It stunned him now to discover that the barber could have actually killed someone.

Staring at her uncle, DeeDee held to silence. She seemed to be completely captivated by his words, yet puzzled.

"DeeDee?'

She raised her brows, her eyes widening to their fullest. "Yes?"

Joshua clasped his hands together. *Give her strength, O Lord.*

"Just before Callie Jean died . . . well, that was the second time I was in El Paso." He took a couple of steps toward her, halting only a foot or so away. "The first time was a little over a year before that."

DeeDee looked away for a moment, her expression pensive. Did she know? Had she guessed?

"She never told me nothin' 'bout her condition. She just let me go off and do what I had to do to earn a livin'. It was just by accident that I found out at all."

"Condition? Found out?"

Joshua watched the tension in DeeDee's posture grow stiffer.

"I was in El Paso, when I seen her crossin' the street . . ." He stopped, sat down on the bed, and swallowed. "She was carryin' a baby. Purtiest lit'l girl I ever seen. As purty as a little red heifer in a flowerbed." He sounded as if he might cry at any moment.

DeeDee looked him directly in the eyes. "What're ya tellin' me, Uncle Zeke?"

Joshua could see by the rigid way she held herself, she did not need to hear the answer.

"I'm sayin' . . ." Zeke reached for her hand, but she would not relinquish her unyielding pose. His Adam's apple bobbed. "I'm sayin' that Aaron and Hedie May ain't yer real pa and ma."

Eyes wide, DeeDee stared at him, shock and fear registering in her features. Slowly at first, she shook her head, then wagged it vehemently. "No! No! This can't be true!"

This time Zeke did grab her hand. "I know it's a lot to swall'r, but it's the gospel."

"You're lyin'!" DeeDee shouted. She blinked hard, and the tears flowed down her cheeks. Her chest heaved with the obvious force of her breathing. "Ya wouldn't do anythin' like that—not you, Uncle Zeke. Why're ya makin' this up?" She tried to pull away, but Zeke held on fast.

"I'm not, girl. It's all the truth—I swear it."

With a visible shiver DeeDee regained a small amount of composure. She stood, then peered down at him. "But why? Why would ya give me to—to—" She paused, then glowered at him. "They *are* your real sister and brother-in-law, aren't they?"

Zeke nodded. His own eyes filled with tears as he rose to face her fully.

"But why, Unc—why?" Her bottom lip quivered. "Why'd ya give me to them? Didn't ya want me? Didn't ya think I'd needed to be with my own—with you?"

"It was the only way," Zeke rushed on with his explanation. "Doin' what I was doin' at the time was no way to bring up a lit'l girl. After Callie Jean died, I was afraid others would come gunnin' for me. I wanted ya to be brought up proper-like and safe. With a woman's influence, and in a proper Christian home. Since Aaron was a preacher, and he and Hedie May was willin' to raise ya, I figgered it was the best place to put ya."

"And what about me?" Snatching her hand out of his grasp, DeeDee backed away, the blue of her eyes shining bright against red rims and tear-soaked lashes. "Did ya ever once consider how *I* might feel about all of this once I grew up and found out ya just gave me away like—like I was pneumonia or somethin'?" She clutched her arms tightly over her middle. "Geez. Ya probably never even planned on tellin' me *ever*, did ya?"

"I did, girl—I swear I did." He took a step toward her.

She backed closer to the window.

Joshua could hardly keep to silence. She looked so forlorn, so hurt, and full of pain. He wanted to run in there and hold her, console her, tell her everything would be all right, and that everything would work out for the best. Yet he did not. It was not his place. Besides, he was not certain if he believed those thoughts himself.

"Please, girl," Zeke pleaded, his tone full of remorse. "Try to understand how it was for me then. A man, a bounty hunter, one gun-draw from death, tryin' to raise a baby girl all by hisself." His body slumped, and his head drooped. There was a catch like a sob in his voice when he spoke again. "I couldn't do that to ya. I had to see ya cared for . . . I loved ya too much to risk yer life stayin' with me."

Joshua watched the great hulk of a man weep. It brought a tear to his own eye, and he could not seem to swallow back a huge lump that had formed in his throat.

Poor Zeke. Under the duress and conditions he had found thrust upon him, he had done the only thing he could to protect DeeDee. Now it was up to her to forgive him, or not.

Joshua shifted his attention from the man now hunched down on the foot of the bed to the sniffling young woman standing in front of the window. Would she? Could she handle this new pain? Could she let it go and accept the love that Zeke offered her now? He sucked in a breath, his own heart aching for her. If ever there was a time when divine intervention was needed, now was that moment.

Hands still clasped tightly together, Joshua lowered his head, touching his brow to his fingers. "Come into her heart, Lord, and let her see how much this man, her true father, loves her," he murmured softly. Above his prayer, he heard DeeDee whimper.

"Oh, Unc—Papa."

He looked up just in time to see her race to Zeke's side and embrace him fiercely.

Falling down to a sitting position beside him, she kissed the man's whiskered cheek. "Ya *did* love me, didn't ya?"

"Oh, girl, if I could only tell ya how much," Zeke said softly, his tone hopeful. "Ya do understand, then?"

Joshua held his breath in anticipation. If DeeDee could not rid herself of the anger she had just shown against Zeke there would be little chance of her staying. And even less of a chance for her and Joshua to fall in love.

He blinked. Where had that come from? Still, the idea felt right. Maybe she *was* the woman God meant for him to be with. Maybe a life with her was the real reason the Lord had brought him to Harmony. Maybe . . . He held himself in check. He could not entertain such thoughts right now. DeeDee and Zeke were the important ones.

DeeDee finally nodded with a smile. Her eyes shone even brighter than before, but this time it was pure radiant joy, not heartache, that visibly spilled out of her. "Oh, yes, Papa. I do understand. And Papa?"

Zeke peered at her with a happy, yet tearstained gaze. "Yes, DeeDee, girl?"

"For everythin' ya went through . . . for everythin' ya did for me . . . I want ya to know . . . I love you."

With that, father and daughter embraced for the first time as a whole and united family.

A tear slipped from Joshua's eye, and he sighed. No matter what the outcome between him and DeeDee, he was truly thankful for the reunion of these two deserving people. For now it was enough that they had finally come together. And for the future? He could only pray steadfastly, and have faith that God's will would be done. . . .

♥
♥ *Chapter 12*

THE FOLLOWING EVENING found DeeDee seated next to Lizzy's bed, reading one of her dime novels, though she found it extremely difficult to concentrate on the story. Her mind was overrun with the discovery that she had been born illegitimate, her true mother was dead, and that the man she had her entire life believed to be her uncle was really her father.

Resting the book in her lap, DeeDee leaned over and stroked the child's brow. And to make matters worse, it was now almost twenty-two hours since Lizzy's accident, and the girl had yet to awaken. With a heavy heart, she sighed. And to think, a little over a week ago she had not even known this small tyke existed. What she would not give to turn back the clock hands and start over in Harmony.

How she would change everything now if she only could.

Joshua's image wavered in her mind. Well, maybe she would not change *everything*, though she would definitely like to alter *some* things, especially those that dealt with the Reverend. She glanced down at the willow-green calico dress she had opted to wear for her visit to the Tollivers'. She fingered the corner of the book.

The dime-novel heroines would never have relinquished her pride and chosen to wear such a garment simply for propriety's sake, but then, DeeDee was not living in the pages of a dime novel. No matter how much she had wanted and tried to imitate the frontier women, she knew it was not fully in her to be that kind of person. She *had* been taught to be a lady, and though she would never admit it aloud, she really did enjoy the feeling the feminine attire offered her.

Besides, just look at what acting callous, ill-tempered, spoiled, and generally obnoxious had gotten her. After only seven days in Harmony she felt cut off from town life. If that were not enough, it seemed Joshua no longer wanted to have anything to do with her, either.

Oh, he had been around. Papa had mentioned talking with him, though Zeke would not say what they had discussed. But DeeDee, herself, had yet to even catch a glimpse of him since she had found out about her birth.

She wanted to talk to Joshua and explain a few things. Tell him that she could no longer be considered as a prospect for a wife in the town's little matchmaking game. And that just as soon as Lizzy was well again, both DeeDee and her father were leaving.

A sharp pain stabbed in her breast. "Funny, how ya never know what ya have till it's ripped away from ya, huh, Lizzy?" she murmured, her gaze washing gently over the little girl's sleeping form. "But I guess in my case, ya could say *I* threw it away, couldn't ya?"

"Threw what away?" Lizzy's mother moved up behind DeeDee.

She flinched. "Mrs. Tolliver. I didn't hear ya come back in."

"I just now returned from the mercantile." The older woman dropped her shawl onto the foot of the bed. "And I'd like it very much if you'd call me Nancy."

"Of course, Nancy." DeeDee smiled appreciatively. She could not believe how understanding the woman was of DeeDee's wanting to be near Lizzy. She was amazed at how receptive Lizzy's mother was of someone who was completely responsible for the child's injury.

"Thanks for sitting with her."

"Did ya get what ya needed at the mercantile?" She moved to rise so that the woman could sit down in her stead.

Shaking her head, Nancy motioned for DeeDee to stay seated. "I didn't really need anything. I just thought you might want some time alone with Lizzy." She peered down at her daughter, then leaned over and caressed her cheek. "Has there been any change?"

"No." DeeDee lifted her gaze from the child to the woman. "Thank you, Nancy," she said after another minute.

"For what?" The woman appeared surprised by the comment.

"For being so understandin', and for not hatin' me the way everybody else does."

The older woman straightened the coverlets around her daughter. "Oh, I don't think everybody really hates you, DeeDee. They just don't know you."

"But you don't really know me any better than anyone else does, and you don't treat me badly." Turning her face downward, DeeDee fought to remain in control of her voice. If Nancy Tolliver was simply hiding feelings of animosity toward DeeDee, she'd just as soon draw it out of the woman and face her now. Lord knows, she deserved it.

"DeeDee." Nancy touched her hand. "I wish you'd quit blaming yourself for this. I don't. It could've happened with anyone watching them—myself included."

"But that's just it," DeeDee said in a very small voice. "I wasn't watchin' them—not like I should've been. Billy Taylor was right."

Bending down, Nancy looked at DeeDee. "You mean you *were* lollygagging around with Reverend Wylie behind the mill?"

"No!" DeeDee nearly shouted. Fearful that she might have disturbed Lizzy, she paused with a glance toward the child. Then, assured she had not, she continued in a lowered tone. "No, I wasn't . . . what ya said. It was like Josh—Reverend Wylie told everybody yesterday on the porch. He wanted to talk to me about what the Ladies' Auxiliary had said."

"I believe you, DeeDee." Nancy smiled, her moss-green eyes reflecting the truth of her words. "Reverend Wylie stopped by later last night and told me the whole story. And though I think the two of you could have chosen a much better time to talk, I do see how it happened. Lord knows, if you don't keep an eye on these children every minute, they're finding a way to get into something— especially Joey."

DeeDee forced a smile and nodded. She held the woman in the greatest respect. Nancy Tolliver was ready for sainthood. "How *is* Joey? I haven't seen him around since—" She darted a gaze at Lizzy. "Since the accident."

"He stays out with the animals mostly." The woman shook her head, a tiny glint of tears in the corners of her eyes. Inhaling deeply, Nancy released it with a sigh. "Never seen that boy do so many chores all at once. But then, he is a little man. Guess concentrating on work is better than sitting her fretting over Lizzy."

DeeDee frowned. "Surely he doesn't think this's his fault?"

The older woman arched a finely shaped brow. "*He* says it was."

"Oh, but that's not true."

Shrugging, Nancy retrieved a rag from a bowl of water on the bedside table. She twisted the cloth, wringing out the liquid, then wiped Lizzy's face. "I tried to tell him that, but he's just a little boy. He doesn't understand that it wasn't anybody's fault."

Rising, DeeDee laid her book down on the nightstand, then peered out the nearby window. "Where is he?"

"Mucking out the milk cow's stall last I saw him."

"Do ya mind if I go talk to him?" DeeDee asked. If she could not do anything for Lizzy right now, maybe she could convince Joey that he had not done anything wrong.

"No, I don't mind," Nancy replied with a small shake of her head. "But, DeeDee?" Reaching out, she grasped hold of DeeDee's hand. "I don't want you heaping all the blame on yourself, either. This was God's will, and nothing more. Maybe it was a lesson for us to pay closer attention to the things that are important, but that's all."

A lesson? God's will? DeeDee had never before thought of anything so devastating as a little girl almost losing her life due to another's negligence as a lesson, nor God's will. She stared at the woman with disbelief.

"You *do* understand what I'm saying?" Nancy punctuated her question with a squeeze to DeeDee's hand.

"I—I'm not sure." Her throat closed.

Nancy smiled. "Well, you go on out there with Joey. You talk to him. Maybe the two of you can figure it out together."

DeeDee nodded. She shot one last glance toward Lizzy. "Ya call me if she stirs, okay?"

"Of course, dear."

Assured the woman would do as DeeDee had requested, she headed for the barn.

"And, dear?"

Hand on the knob, DeeDee pulled the door open, then halted. She peered back at Nancy Tolliver.

"While you're out there trying to convince Joey that it wasn't his fault . . . you reassure yourself the same about you, all right?"

Hesitating a moment, DeeDee swallowed back the emotional lump that leaped into her throat, then bobbed her head. Without further delay, she headed outside. Yes. Nancy Tolliver was definitely headed for sainthood.

Heading down the dirt road to the Tolliver house, Joshua kicked a small stone ahead of him. He thought back to the evening that DeeDee had arrived in town, and how the two of them had played kick-the-rock that night. He had been intrigued by her from the first moment they had met. She was smart and witty, funny and most charming in her own defiant, headstrong, obtrusive, and provoking sort of way.

He shook his head. Now that she had entered upon their lives, however did the people of Harmony think they would get along without her? Nothing had been the same since her arrival. The town might be renowned for the bright hues of its buildings, but DeeDee's lively spirit was brighter than them all. If she decided to leave, the town would never be the same.

A cold shiver raced up his spine. He stiffened against its intrusion. It reminded him of the sunburn that still plagued his back . . . the day's events that occurred with the blistering.

DeeDee's defenseless expression wavered in his mind. Lord help him, she had felt so good in his arms that day. She had looked so beautiful with those yellow speckles of paint freckling across the bridge of her little nose. And her autumn hair . . . it had glistened like morning-misted leaves in the fall.

Like an ungovernable breeze, a shudder whipped through his body. No. He was not about to let this happen. He had to convince DeeDee to stay. He had talked to Zeke. He had confessed to the older man that he had overheard the incidents concerning DeeDee's birth.

During the course of their conversation, Zeke had told Joshua of the family's plans for leaving for San Francisco just as soon as the barbershop-dentist office could be sold. He had already put a For Sale sign in the window of his shop.

Joshua had tried to make him see reason, tried to talk the man into staying—into persuading DeeDee to stay in Harmony. But it had been useless energy spent.

"Ye've got me convinced, Parson," Zeke had said. "It's DeeDee ye've got to contend with. And that ain't goin' to be easy. When that girl makes up her mind 'bout somethin', she's so obstinate she wouldn't move camp for a prairie fire."

Smirking, Joshua shook his head. He kicked the rock a few yards ahead. How drab and boring Harmony would become if it were to lose *both* DeeDee and Zeke. *They* were definitely two of the true colors of the town, and it was about time somebody made it a point to inform a few people of that fact.

But for now, that would have to wait. He had to talk to DeeDee first and make her see reason. If he could not talk her into staying, there was no sense in pursuing the notion with the townsfolk.

Coming upon the Tolliver yard, he caught sight of her going into the barn—at least, he thought it was her. She was not outfitted in any of her usual frontier garb. Instead, she wore a most attractive green dress. He squinted after her. Was that really DeeDee Gallagher?

In the evening's waning light the woman's hair appeared to be the same fiery shade of autumn. The determined stride was the same. Still—why was she not decked out in buckskin and homespun?

Curiosity marking his pace, he crossed to the barn, then moved around to an open window. He peeked inside.

Joey Tolliver sat on a stool, head plowed into the side of the family milk cow, hands yanking mercilessly on the animal's engorged teats.

"Hi, Joey," DeeDee said with a smile. She stepped inside the stall and moved up closer to the little boy. "Ya mind if I keep ya company for a little while?"

Halting his chore for only a second, Joey answered with a slight uplift of his shoulders.

Apparently, DeeDee took that as a positive sign. After pulling a bale of hay nearer the child, she sat down and cleared her throat. "Your mother tells me ye've been workin' awful hard lately."

Joshua could tell by the forced cheerfulness of her voice that she was nervous. Cautiously, he moved around to the barn door and entered. He wanted to be there for the two of them in case DeeDee needed some help talking to the child. He halted just inside and waited.

DeeDee looked up, but did not speak to him before she returned her attention to Joey.

The boy did not reply.

Hesitating a moment, she began anew. "Joey, we need to talk." Another pause.

No response.

"It's not good ya should go on blamin' yerself for what happened to yer sister," she blurted out.

Milk pinged into the bucket, but Joey remained silent.

Even in the dim lantern-light filling the stall, Joshua could see the mark of frustration mounting in DeeDee's expression.

He thought of part of his favorite Bible passage. Ecclesiastes three one through eight: " . . . there is a time to every purpose under the heaven." No, whatever spiritual comfort became of this, he felt certain it was best left to the two of them.

"Please, Joey, won't ya take a few minutes to listen to me?" DeeDee pleaded, her voice sounding shaky.

"I kin hear ya," he said, his tone tight.

Swallowing, DeeDee appeared to gather her thoughts. With tearful eyes, she glanced at Joshua, hesitated another moment, then peered back at the boy. "It wasn't yer fault yer sister was hurt," she reiterated.

The milk squirted into the pail, making a splashing sound, but the boy did not acknowledge DeeDee's conclusion.

"If it was anyone's fault, it was mine," she insisted. "*I* was the one watchin' the two of ya." She paused again, subjecting her bottom lip to a gnashing of her teeth. "And ya know what, Joey?"

He did not answer. He just yanked on that poor cow's udders harder.

"I'm not even certain than anyone's truly to blame." She pulled her lip between her teeth, then released it. "It might just be that this was a lesson of some kind—a painful one, I'll grant ya—but a lesson just the same."

He slowed his movements, but only for a second, before returning to his task.

She shot another look at Joshua, her expression filled with pain. He offered her a reassuring smile, then nodded. Could it be that the Lord had finally gotten through to DeeDee? Did she truly believe there *was* a purpose to everything?

"Maybe God in his infinite wisdom chose to make the two of us more aware of the things we hold precious. Maybe he just wants us to pay more attention to the things we have, and not always go lookin' for greater adventures than what we can find in our own yards." She stopped short and blinked. Did she, herself, hear what she had just said?

Joshua sent a hopeful prayer heavenward.

"Ya ain't makin' no sense," Joey spouted. "What's Lizzy gettin' hurt got to do with adventures, and lessons, and such?"

"Well—I don't know for sure, but—" DeeDee looked at him imploringly.

Joshua remained silent. He could not say anything to the boy any better than what DeeDee had.

When he did not speak, DeeDee returned her attention to Joey.

"Maybe if we *really* search out our hearts—both of us—maybe we'll discover the answer. What d'ya think?"

Slowly Joey stilled his movements.

The cow rolled her eyes toward him.

After a drawn-out moment he finally lifted his head and looked at DeeDee.

She smiled. Her brows lifted, and she peered at him with eyes filled with expectation.

Turning fully around on his stool, Joey faced DeeDee. "Ya mean I mightn't ought to be so all-fired stubborn about doin' ever'thing the big kids do? Like wantin' to climb that mill wheel?"

Joshua moved into the shadows. He did not want the boy to see him. DeeDee was doing fine without him.

Tears forming in her eyes, DeeDee nodded. "If they were to jump into a nest of rat'lers, and said it was fun, would you?"

Joshua watched the profile of Joey's features turn wide-eyed fearful. "Shucks, no! That's just dad-blamed dumb. Them snakes would kill ya dead-certain—" His expression brightened to one of sudden realization.

DeeDee covered her mouth with trembling fingers.

Apparently, the boy had understood her meaning. "I still don't see how Lizzy's gettin' hurt teaches me a lesson," he said in a doubtful tone.

"I'm not sure, either," DeeDee said after taking a deep breath. "But maybe—just maybe—ya might want to enjoy your sister's company a little more than ya do."

Joey shrugged, then spun back to his milking. "She's okay—when the older boys ain't around."

DeeDee grabbed his arm and turned him to face her again. "That's just it, Joey. Ya only like her when there's no one else to play with."

"That ain't so. . . . I like her fine. It's just that she—she—"

"Stutters?" DeeDee finished.

"Yeah. See, ya noticed, too. Ever'body does." Joey poked out his bottom lip. "The other kids make fun of her."

"And how does that make *you* feel?"

He shrugged. "I dunno. It bothers me some, but what kin I do about it? They're a whole bunch bigger'n I am."

"Ya can stick up for her when they tease her. Ya can play with her when they won't. Ya can be a big brother to her, and help her learn to speak better."

"But it's a 'fliction. There ain't no help for it."

"That's not true, Joey." DeeDee almost sounded angry. "With patience, love, and a lot of help, Lizzy can learn to speak just as well as anybody else."

Joey tipped his head to one side. "Quit foolin' around, DeeDee. It ain't funny."

"I don't mean for it to be."

"Really?" The boy still sounded skeptical.

DeeDee grinned. "Cross my heart," she said, drawing the sign on her chest. "I promised Lizzy I'd teach her to read—better than you, if she worked real hard."

"Ya know, I think I'd be right proud to have her read better'n me, too."

"Good." DeeDee's whole demeanor appeared to brighten.

This was the first positive sign Joshua had seen from either DeeDee or Joey since Lizzy had been hurt.

"I brought some books with me, some stories, other schoolbooks, if you'd like to read some of them to Lizzy," DeeDee suggested.

"She's awake?" Joey all but leaped up from his perch on the stool.

"No—no." DeeDee grabbed his elbow and pulled him back to her. "Not yet, but she will be soon."

Joey's shoulders slumped. He thrust out his bottom lip. "Then why'd ya say I should read to her?"

"She can hear ya. Even though she's sleepin', she can still hear ya," DeeDee assured him with a wink.

"Honest?" He did not sound as though he truly believed her.

"Yep. Matter of fact—" She tugged out a sprig of hay from the boy's hair. "Why don't we hurry up with this milkin' project ya got goin' and run in there and see if we can't pick out somethin' special to read to her."

"Somethin' that'll wake her up?" Joey suddenly displayed some enthusiasm.

"Yeah, hon. Somethin' that'll wake her up. But first—" She slipped her hand down to his. "About what we were talkin' about earlier."

"Huh?" Obviously, the child had already forgotten the subject DeeDee had initially specified.

"You know, about blamin' yerself?"

"Oh, yeah." Joey's shoulders drooped.

"Well, now, I meant what I said earlier." She straightened the boy's shirt and suspenders. "I don't want ya to go around mopin' anymore, and thinkin' it was yer fault, okay? 'Cause it wasn't."

"Okay," he said, albeit with a look of reluctance. "'Cause it was a lesson from God, right?"

"Right." She smiled, her eyes glistening with moisture.

"Well . . ." He stared at her a moment, his expression marking a possible change in decision. "I won't . . . if you won't."

After another few seconds of apparent deliberation, DeeDee finally submitted to his arrangement with a nod.

Joshua watched the woman and child hug each other fiercely. Whether or not she had believed her own words, she had at least convinced the boy of the truth. Turning away from the scene, he eased out of the barn.

He was deeply impressed with the way DeeDee had eased Joey's fears of being responsible for his sister's accident. Now, if only Joshua could alleviate his own guilt about the same incident. After all, if he had not pushed DeeDee into leaving the children alone on the riverbank, Lizzy would not have gotten hurt.

A voice inside his heart softened the blame. *Remember the woman's words. It is naught but a lesson. The child will recover.*

Clinging to his faith, Joshua rounded the barn and turned back for Harmony. He had to believe that Lizzy would be all right. *If you expect a miracle, then you shall receive one.* They were Reverend Harkington's words, and as far back as Joshua could remember, they had always been true words.

The sun had long since relinquished its reign of the sky, yielding the earth to the moon's dusky rule.

It was a little slower going for Joshua to return to the boardinghouse in the dark, but he managed the way without any problem. In fact, it had taken him nearly an hour and a half to travel the distance from the Tolliver farm to Harmony, but the time had seemed to actually pass very quickly.

His mind was full of a new plan—a way he might be able to persuade the Gallaghers to stay—not to mention teach the good, Christian townsfolk a lesson of their own. Hadn't DeeDee told Joey that events such as accidents were God's will? That they were the Lord's way of warning his children to pay heed and learn from the lesson?

That was when the idea—the device he was going to use—sparked in Joshua's brain. Entering the boardinghouse, he made a hasty ascent to his room. He could hardly wait to get started drafting out his scheme on paper.

The only difference with Joshua's impending message and reproof was that the method of teaching *his* lesson would by no means be an accident. Everything he was planning would be done intentionally, and he thoroughly expected to enjoy every single element he would say and do.

# ♥ Chapter 13

SITTING AT HIS desk in his room, Joshua set down his pen and rubbed his eyes. He had been working since he had returned from the Tolliver home just after sunset, and now, several hours later, he was growing fatigued. He picked up his pocket watch from the corner of the writing table and checked the time. Eleven twenty-seven.

He clamped the cover closed, then, winding the stem, he peered at the papers before him. Would his plan work? He would need help if he were going to manage to pull it off without any trouble. He scooted the chair back a space, leaned down and untied his shoes, then, each in turn, tugged them off.

Who could he get to aid him? Inside his socks he wiggled his toes. The scheme was to teach the community a lesson. If he involved someone in town, chances were it would be known to all before the chosen moment.

Zeke. Maybe Joshua could get him to help. He had the humor for it, that was for certain. And it was only too apparent that the man had no tolerance for how the townsfolk were treating his—

Joshua stumbled over the thought. He shook his head. He could no longer think of DeeDee as Zeke's niece. She was the man's daughter. What a kettle of fish *this* would turn out to be once the citizen's of Harmony made the discovery. And Joshua knew they would. It was only a matter of time—and a short time at that. Already people were asking questions and snooping into the reason for Zeke wanting to sell his shop and move, and the man had only put the For Sale sign up that morning.

But if Joshua's strategy worked . . . He sent another of many quick prayers heavenward. If his plan worked, then once the news of who DeeDee truly was came out, nothing would come of it. All of Harmony might, and in all probability would, be shocked, but at least the gossip would be remain at a minimum. And, maybe—just maybe—Zeke and DeeDee would not leave.

He took a deep breath, then lolled his head backward, rolling it gently from side to side against his neck and shoulders. He was tired, but he was too keyed up to fall asleep just yet. Hot milk might help him relax. He checked the time again, then listened for any movements in the large house.

Minnie and Maisie had long since gone to bed.

But what about Ruth Alice and Rebecca? Sometimes, weather permitting, they would spend long hours visiting on the back porch.

He had been so engrossed in detailing his scheme, he had not heard either one come up to their rooms, and right now he had no desire to be confronted by either of them. It seemed that no matter where he went or what he did, one or the other of the two women was always around.

Standing, he quietly crossed the floor to the door, then, silently as he could, pulled it ajar. He strained his hearing, listening for female chatter or light tittering.

Nothing. All remained undisturbed.

He opened the door fully, then stepped into the hall, concealing his exit by quietly shutting the door behind him. Tiptoeing, he made his way down the stairs. He halted in the vestibule and gave his attention to any sounds in the house.

As before, nothing stirred.

Good. The young women had gone to bed as he had hoped.

He relaxed a little, then proceeded to the kitchen. Dusky moonbeams cast just enough light through the single window over the washboard for Joshua to make his way around the interior. Once inside the cookroom, he gathered the metal pitcher of milk and a pan from the pantry, then checked the woodstove.

The flame inside was only a glow of embers, but the top remained hot. It would be enough to heat his drink.

He poured an ample amount of milk into the small pot, set it down, then placed the cool urn on the work surface. Stretching, he braced his spine with hands, then, with guarded effort, arched backward. The sunburn still ached a little, but he forced himself to ignore the pain.

He thought of the papers lying on his desk. Usually, it took nearly an entire week to plan his sermons, but not this time. He could not believe how quickly he had written the oration. And it had been fun, too. Now all he had to do was memorize it. He hoped that would not be too difficult.

Remembering how DeeDee had touted his practice sermon in the meadow, he smiled. *I'll try to do your praise justice,* he thought. Would his plan please her? He hoped so. He was going to do this for her. He gave himself a mental shake. He had to be truthful. He was going to do this for *himself,* too. It was something he had always wanted, but how would it be received by the congregation?

Standing in the dark, he leaned on the counter and shrugged to himself. They would either accept it or not. Reverend Harkington had told Joshua to make this parish his own. Now was his chance.

It had taken him a long time, and a lot of prodding by his conscience and DeeDee, of course, but he had finally decided to do it.

The front door squeaked open.

Joshua tensed.

Silence reigned. Yet there was something—a presence. Someone had entered the house. The door had not opened of its own accord.

Then he heard it.

Light footsteps approached. A shadow moved into the kitchen.

Someone sighed.

Joshua squinted into the dim moonlight. It was not until a familiar silhouette passed in front of the window that he recognized the person.

Rubbing her neck, DeeDee sauntered across the opposite side of the room. She stopped in front of the sideboard and retrieved a glass, then filled it with water from the pump.

Joshua remained immobile, watching as the woman drank with greedy gulps, exhaling with loud, unladylike breaths into the container. He should say something—let her know that he was there, but he had no wish to startle her.

Staring at her outline back-draped in moonbeams, he smiled. Even in the darkness she was beautiful. He relaxed again, resting against the counter. This was something he had never before experienced. True, he had observed her in the past without her knowledge, but never in the intimacy of a shadowy room.

She set the glass down, but remained poised in front of the window looking out.

He allowed his gaze to travel over the shadowy contours of her very feminine shape, indulging his senses in a moment of purely masculine admiration. He basked in the return of the emotions that always stirred him whenever he indulged himself with thoughts of the woman in his fantasies. His body stirred with the heat of raw desire. His heartbeat quickened, and his mouth went dry.

Observing her in the veil of darkness like this was even more stimulating to his imagination than the light of day. At this minute he did not think of himself as a minister, but rather a man—plain and simple. He swallowed, his gaze following her every movement.

As if in slow motion, she pulled her braid over one shoulder, and untwisted it. Then flipping it backward, she reached up and shook the mass, gliding her hands downward through its length.

Joshua's stomach tightened. He knew Delilah Gallagher was a mortal woman by her spoken word and the very real touch of her skin. Yet, if ever a human female could be held in reference as a perfect piece of the Lord's work, this one could. If ever he had doubted it before, by her existence alone he now knew God had brought the two of them to Harmony for a special purpose. He fought hard to keep his thoughts from turning lustful. Still, he was a man. The feelings he was experiencing were natural, were they not?

She released a little sigh and stretched. Then stilled, yet did not.

What was she doing? Joshua became entranced.

She appeared to be doing something to her neck, or maybe the bodice of her gown. She pumped the water again, dipped her hands into the liquid, and patted her throat. Suddenly she pulled the garment open.

Joshua flinched. No. He could not let her do that.

At that moment the milk began to sizzle on the stove.

Inwardly he groaned. He had all but forgotten about the drink he had been preparing before she had entered the kitchen.

"Who's that?" Snatching the front of her dress closed, she whipped around and sniffed the air. "Is someone there?" Her voice shook.

Joshua cleared his throat. There was no help for matters now. She knew he was there. "It's me, DeeDee. Joshua."

"What—" She lowered her tone. "What're *you* doin' lurkin' around down here? I thought everyone was in bed by now."

"I wasn't *lurking*—I was working late." He crossed to the stove, trying to sound nonchalant. "I thought some hot milk might help me rest." He kept a watchful eye on her.

"Oh," she said, hurrying to rebutton her dress. She sniffed again. "Smells like it's scorched."

He nodded, though he knew she probably could not see him. "I think you're right." Taking the pan, he moved to the side door, opened it, and tossed out the liquid, then quietly reclosed the door. He stepped up beside her and pumped some water into the pan for cleaning.

"Hot milk, hmm?" she questioned with an arched brow. Fully awash in the moon's light, her face beamed bright and strangely alluring.

His breath caught. Afraid of taking a chance on a shaky voice, he nodded. He inhaled sharply. What was that fragrance? She always smelled outdoorsy clean, but this was different. Almost flowery. Like . . . a rain-washed meadow of wildflowers? Strange. He had never before detected any perfumed scent from her. Why was she wearing toilet water tonight? For him? His vanity pricked him sorely. How could that be? She had not even known he was awake.

"Here," she said after the unguarded moment. "Let me do that." Taking the pot from him, she scrubbed it clean, then rinsed it out in the basin.

"I'll get more milk," Joshua offered. He had to do something to distract his wayward thoughts. He hurried to the counter next to the stove and retrieved the metal pitcher.

"Ya know, hot milk does sound pretty good right now. I think I'll have some, too. Would ya mind gettin' an extra mug?"

"Sure thing."

DeeDee giggled softly.

"What?" He handed her the milk, then, after taking down two cups from the sideboard, he set them on the work surface.

"Oh, I was just thinkin' what a truly bad influence I've been on you."

Folding his arms across his chest, Joshua frowned. "How do you mean?" Surely the woman had not known he had been staring at her in the darkness?

She chuckled again. "Any other time, if anyone had asked ya to get them somethin', you'd have said 'of course' or 'it would be a pleasure,' but 'sure thing'?" She shook her head. "That sounds like somethin' *I'd* say."

Joshua joined in on her soft laughter. He shrugged. "I guess you're right about that. You *are* a bad influence."

With his agreement she appeared to stiffen a little. Crossing in front of him, she returned the pot to the stove.

The air seemed to thicken a bit.

What had he said? He had only agreed with her. He had not meant it, though. "Um—how's Lizzy?" he said, trying to lighten the moment.

"Oh!" She whipped around to face him. "Actually, I'm glad ye're not asleep. Lizzy woke up a couple of hours ago."

Joshua grinned. His spirit lifted. "Thank the Lord!" he said in earnest praise.

"Yeah, the doc was really startin' to get worried when she didn't wake up after so long."

"How is she? Has the doctor seen her yet? Is she all right?"

DeeDee nodded. "Mmm-hmm. We sent Joey for him as soon as Lizzy spoke." Moving to the only stool in the room, she climbed onto it, then, very ladylike, straightened the skirt of her dress. "The little imp nearly scared the life out of me."

Joshua blinked with surprise. "How'd she do that?"

"Well, Joey had just finished readin' her a story from one of my books, and while his mother was puttin' him to bed, I was straightenin' Lizzy's sheet around her."

"I don't understand." He shook his head trying to figure out how straightening bedsheets would cause the little girl to frighten DeeDee.

"I'm gettin' to that." She gestured him to silence with a flash of her palms. "She must've been awake a few minutes, 'cause when I looked up from what I was doin', there she was, just layin' there wide awake, starin' at me like some old hoot-owl." She chuckled again.

"I bet that was a little unnerving," Joshua agreed.

"Yeah, and ya wanna know what was the first thing she said?"

"What?"

Pinching the fabric of her gown, she held it up as if it were a dirty rag. "She wanted to know why I was dressed so funny."

Joshua laughed out loud.

"Shh." She held her finger to her lips, but an uncontrollable snicker escaped her. "You'll wake everybody."

Regaining his composure, he arched a jovial brow. "You thought it was funny, too."

Still pressing her finger to her mouth, she nodded, another titter escaping in a broken hiss. "Yeah, well, most people would've thought what I have on *is* proper, but not that little one."

"Well, she's right." He gestured toward the garment. "It is a little unusual for you."

She nodded, but her mood seemed to sober again.

What was wrong? Had she been offended by his comment? Surely not. She had laughed, too. He tipped his head to one side and peered more closely at her, but in the dimness of the light, it was hard to read her expression. "Is there something you're not telling me? Something with Lizzy?"

She shook her head. "No, not with Lizzy."

"But there is something?" He was starting to get really concerned.

"There's something I want to talk to ya about, yeah."

At that moment Joshua remembered the milk. He held up a hand. "Hold your thought. Let me get the milk before it burns again." He turned and picked up the mugs, then poured the liquid. He handed a cup to her. Then, after returning to his former position against the counter, he took a sip and swallowed. "Now, I'm ready."

DeeDee sampled her drink. She took a huge breath and released it with a sigh. "There's no nice way to say this," she began all at once. "So I might as well just blurt it out."

"All right. I'm listening." What could be so bad that she was having this much trouble saying it?

"I'm sorry, Joshua, but I can no longer be included as a contender in your contest to find a wife."

Joshua nearly dropped his mug. He was so stunned, his mouth fell agape. "My—my what?"

He blinked, then set his cup down. Had he heard her correctly?

"Please don't make this any harder," she said, shifting nervously on the stool.

"Harder than what?" He stared at her. For the life of him, he could not figure out what she was talking about. "I have no idea what you mean. What's all this about you being a contender in some game? And for a wife?" He had not even gotten his house built. How could she believe that he was looking for a wife?

"Look, I'm really flattered that ya would even include me with Ruth Alice and Rebecca, but—"

"Wait a minute!" He held up his hands. "Are you telling me what I think you're telling me?" He did not wait for her to reply. His mind reeled, and he tried to sort through the fog of disbelief clouding his thoughts. "Are you saying there's some kind of competition going on with you, Ruth Alice, and Rebecca as rivals, and me as the prize?"

DeeDee pierced him with a questioning stare. "Well, I wouldn't exactly put it like that—but yeah." She nodded. "I guess that about sums it up."

Joshua froze, stock-still. He could not believe it. How had this happened? He had never even suggested to anyone that he might be interested in either of the women. True, someone might have guessed that he was attracted to DeeDee, but Ruth Alice?

He always enjoyed listening to her sing. And even though Rebecca was one of the prettiest women he had ever met, and her knowledge of the Bible was astonishing at times, Joshua had never considered either of them as anything but a friend.

"Joshua, I'm sorry," DeeDee repeated. "But in light of some things that I've recently learned about myself—Joshua?" Leaning forward, she frowned. "Are ya listenin' to me?"

Slowly he reclaimed reality. "I'm sorry, what did you say?" He was still in shock.

"I said—"

"Hold it." He stood up straight. "How is it that you think I'm looking for a wife? And how did all of you come into play as my marriage prospects?"

"Joshua, please, ya act like this's the first time ye've heard of all of this."

He nodded. "It is."

Narrowing her line of vision on him, her expression was one of bewilderment. "Quit foolin' around."

"I'm not," he insisted.

"Ye're serious?" Her brows shot up. "But I thought—"

"Look, DeeDee, I don't know how all of this got started, or who told you I was in the process of seeking a wife, but—"

"It was Miss Minnie and Miss Maisie."

"What?" Joshua could feel his temper flare.

DeeDee bobbed her head. "And Unc—Pa—I mean—" She shook her head, her eyes widening. "It was Zeke, too."

"Zeke?" Joshua shook his head. Surely she was mistaken. He could well believe that the twin matrons might start such a rumor, and even plot to see him married, but Zeke? No. It could not be true.

"I only just found out about my part in all of this the other day," DeeDee confessed, her voice connoting innocence. "He told me about the match-making game the two women had plotted, and how Maisie had chosen Rebecca as her competitor, and Minnie had sent for her favorite niece, Ruth Alice, as her choice—"

"So how did you get involved? I suppose Zeke thought with you being a minister's daughter, you'd be an even better selection?"

Appearing as if she were in a trance, she only nodded.

"I see. So that's why you came to Harmony? To hopefully marry me?" He was growing angrier by the second. And to think he had wanted to please and help this woman, and all the while she was scheming for a proposal.

She scowled. "No. I told ya. I just found out myself last Sunday."

Of course she had. Now that he thought about it, all of his so called *accidents* involving her were a bit coincidental. He folded his arms over his chest. His temples throbbed furiously. "And you expect me to believe that?"

"It's true, Joshua."

He stared at her with insulted scorn. If only he were a different man, he would grab her by the shoulders and throttle her within an inch of her life. How could she have been a party to this humiliation?

"Look, Joshua." By her sneering tone, it was evident that she, too, was becoming irritated. "I didn't like this little game any more than you apparently do."

"And so, of course, that's why you agreed to try and ensnare me with your wiles."

"Wiles?" she shrieked. Leaping down from her seat, she slammed the cup onto the countertop, then shoved a finger in his face. "Listen here, Joshua Wylie. I *never* did anything of the kind. I'm tellin' ya for the last time. *I didn't know anything about this little matchmakin' game till the other day.*"

Joshua glared at her. How was he supposed to believe her? "So you're telling me that you weren't after my attention?"

She shook her head.

"Or that your knocking me into the trough that first day wasn't just a female ploy?"

She scrunched her face up into a tight pucker. "Why, you swolled-up, mud-slingin'—" Apparently reluctant to actual put a name to her description of him, she gritted her teeth and growled instead.

He flinched. Why was *she* getting angry? *He* was the one that had been duped.

"I never had *any* intentions of marrying you!"

"If that's true, then why did you wait until now to tell me about all of this?" He was not about to let her turn this around on him.

Her features still held rigid, she planted her hands on her hips. "Because I didn't want ya to be disappointed with me when ya found out I was a—that Uncle—I mean—Oh, geez!" She threw up her hands. "Zeke Gallagher is my father."

What did that have to do with any of this? "I know."

"And—" She thrust her arms into a folded position across her stomach. "My papa and mother were never married, either."

Seeing the defiant sincerity in her expression, he softened toward her. He had remembered how devastated she had been to learn about the truth of her birth, and he knew it had taken a lot of courage for her to divulge this information to him—mad or not. "I know," he said quietly.

"And I wouldn't—" She batted her eyes as if coming out of a hypnotic state of mind. "What did you say?"

"I know about your mother."

"Ya do?"

"Zeke told me. He also told me that he was your true father."

After a moment of hesitation she shifted so that she did not fully face him. "And?" she challenged.

He shrugged. "There's no *and*. He just told me, that's all."

"Good." She seemed to relax a little, though her features still held a smug appearance. Her demeanor switched to curiosity. "Why?"

"I guess he just wanted me to know." Without thought he slipped back to his original accusation.

"He probably thought I should know the truth if I was going to consider you for marriage."

"Look, I told ya, I had no intentions of marryin'—"

"If that's true, why did you let me kiss you the other night?" He lowered his voice to a sly tone.

Instantly, visibly, she tensed. She shot a look around the room before returning a cool, intent stare to him. "Ya know somethin', Joshua?"

"What?" Would she actually confess her attraction to him? If she would just meet him on level ground, everything else would be forgiven, and it would certainly make his own admission easier.

"I think ye're about as conceited as a barber's cat." She wheeled away, then spun back. "*If* he had one."

He pulled back with a start. What was that supposed to mean? He did not have time to ponder the question. "DeeDee, stop." He could not let her leave just yet. He still had some explaining of his own to do. "Look, I'm sorry. I think I know you well enough to know that you're not lying about this matchmaking game."

Looking him straight in the eye, she lifted her chin.

"It's just that, well, I didn't know anything about it, and well . . . I was surprised."

"Is that suppose to make me feel better?" Obviously, *she* did not want to make this easy on him.

"Please," he said, gesturing her back to the stool. "Now I've got some things I want to tell you."

"Like what?" she asked, taking her seat as he had offered her.

He scratched his head. If he wanted her to stay in Harmony, he was going to have to tell her everything about himself. And the sooner, the better. He inhaled. Here goes. "You're not the only one whose parents weren't married." Pausing, he glanced away, then looked back at her.

She appeared unmoved.

"I grew up in an orphanage in Syracuse, New York, not even knowing who my parents were. A piece of paper with my name, and a twenty-dollar gold piece tucked inside the blanket I was wrapped in, was my only inheritance."

"So ye're a bas—I mean, ye're illegitimate, too?" Her eyes rounded. Her voice softened.

He nodded. "Ironic, isn't it?"

She frowned. "I don't follow ya."

"It seems Zeke might have known what was best for us, after all. Maybe we really *are* suited for each other."

"Oh, no." She held up a hand, and shook her head. "I told ya."

He moved closer, halting at her knees. Reaching up to her face, he caressed her cheek. He had to test his theory that maybe she was attracted to him as much as he was to her. "So the other night didn't mean anything to you?"

"Joshua, don't." She shrugged his hand away, then tried to get off the stool.

Stepping in her way, he reached around and gripped the cutting board on either side of her.

"Answer me, DeeDee." He could not back down now. He had to know. He brushed her lips with his.

She trembled against his touch. "I don't think this's a good idea, Joshua. I'm—" She swallowed, glanced at his mouth, then swallowed again.

It was a sure giveaway. At least he hoped it was. "You're what?" If he pressed her for an answer while she was vulnerable, maybe she would give in to the truth and admit her interest in him. He leaned forward and tasted her lips again.

She shuddered, her breath an unmistakable sigh against his kiss.

He took the yearning sound as an invitation. His blood heated. His gaze swept her flushed face. His pulse leaped. Testing her further, he slipped one hand down to her waist, then grazed the fullness of her bottom lip with his tongue.

She closed her eyes and leaned her head back, yielding her mouth to his. Shyly her tongue touched his, searing his flesh, catching him as off guard as he had hoped to do with her. Suddenly she jumped. Her hand flew to his chest, pushing. "We can't, Joshua," she said breathlessly.

Puzzled, he searched the delicate contours of her face. "Why not?" he asked, his own voice just as shaky.

She swallowed again. "Because—" She gently shoved him farther away. "As soon as Papa can sell the shop, we're moving to San Francisco."

Joshua's heart clamped tight on a beat. His hopes crumbled. "Why? You *do* feel something for me—I know you do." He was not going to give up without a fight.

"It doesn't matter what I feel."

"The hell it doesn't!"

DeeDee flinched. "Joshua."

"Forgive me, DeeDee, but am I to assume you're really not in love with me?"

"In love with you?" She stared at him openly.

He nodded. "Are you telling me you aren't? Are you saying that this is all one-sided?"

Her eyes flew wide. "One-sided?"

Joshua could not believe what he had just said. Until that very moment he had not fully entertained the thought himself, and now he had practically confessed his own love for her. Practically? He had.

Though she smiled, she shook her head, then slipped out of his embrace. "I'm flattered, Joshua. And no, I'm not sayin' I don't feel things . . . wondrous things for you, but love?" She looked away, before peering back at him. "I just can't think of ya like that anymore. I'm leavin' soon." She started for the kitchen door. "It's for the best, really."

The heck it was. He could not allow this to happen—not now—when he was so close. "All right." He raised his voice.

Faltering on a step, she turned back to him.

"All right," he said again, this time softer. His mind struggled for something to say that would make her want to stay. "Can you just tell me why?"

She shrugged. "There's too much against us. The town would be happy to see me on the next train goin' anywhere. And even if that weren't a problem, what d'ya think would happen when they find out that Zeke's really my father? And especially if you and I were to truly get serious about each other?"

He groaned inwardly. He *was* serious. He just had not acknowledged that fact to himself before tonight. "DeeDee, I've been attracted to you from the first moment I met you. I think you have with me, too." He paused again, hoping she would confirm his suspicions.

She did not. She just stared at him.

Still grasping a thread of hope, he rushed on. "And now that I know how I feel—I just can't let you go."

"Joshua." She moved nearer and stroked his jaw. "We can't fight facts. And the fact is, someone like me—someone named Delilah—someone that talks the way I do and acts the way I do, could never be married to someone as wonderful as you. It's a timeless curse brought down on the name from the original Delilah. And no matter how I feel, it just wouldn't work for us. The town—the people—wouldn't let it."

"We could move." He was grasping at anything he could think of.

She shook her head, her eyes misting with tears. "It wouldn't be different in another town." Still shaking her head, she moved back for the door.

"DeeDee?" he called, halting her at the threshold.

She peered back at him, her expression sorrowful. "What?"

He had to get some kind of answer from her. He had to know. "I wasn't imagining it all this time, was I? About us, I·mean? I was right about how you feel about me?" He held his breath, awaiting her reply.

She did not answer right away. She hovered in the doorway another minute. Then, with a movement, he almost missed, she lifted her chin and brought it down.

His heart slammed against his chest. He grinned. He knew it had to have been true. But what good did it do him now? He had found out too late. She was leaving—unless . . . He thought of the scheme he had been working on upstairs.

Pulling her gaze from his, DeeDee took a step forward.

"DeeDee?"

Her shoulders sagged. "Don't, Joshua. Ye're only making it harder . . . on both of us."

Good. Then he still had a chance. "When're you leaving?"

"I don't know," she answered without facing him. "Papa wants to sell the shop first. He's got a buyer comin' in to look at it in the mornin', so I guess whenever the next train comes in."

Joshua searched his mind. If his memory of the schedule was correct, that would be two days from now. No, that would not do. It was too soon. "Could—" His voice faltered with renewed excitement. "Could you do me a favor and wait until after Sunday? I have a surprise for you."

"Joshua—"

"Please, DeeDee. Just this one thing. I've been planning it all night, and I think you're especially going to like it."

That caught her attention. Looking back at him, she squinted, apparently trying to figure his reasoning. "What're ya up to, Joshua?"

He shrugged, then shoved his fingertips into his pants pockets. "It's a surprise." He pushed for an answer. "So, will you?"

Again, she delayed her reply. Then, finally, she smiled. One brow vaulted. "We'll see." Then, without another sound, she made her escape up to her room.

This time Joshua did not try to stop her. He had too much to think about—too much to consider. He glanced at the cup of milk he had left on the counter. No, he no longer wanted anything that would make him sleep. Coffee. That was what he needed now.

He headed for the pantry. He had a lot of reworking to do on his plans if he was going to succeed. And only three days to pull everything he needed to do together, if he was going to be able to achieve his goal—and make his lesson a reality.

# ♥ ♥ Chapter 14

DEEDEE AWOKE EARLY Sunday morning to a bright and sunshiny day, yet *she* did not feel nearly as radiant. She and her father were leaving Harmony later today. The train was due in at 2 P.M. By midnight they would be in Wichita, two days later, Dodge City, and from there . . .

Poised in front of the bureau mirror, she finished brushing her hair, plaited it, then twisted it in a fashionable upsweep and pinned it to her head. She sighed, her heart heavy. She did not want to think about where they would go from there. Still, it *was* what she wanted to do—at least, it was what she *thought* she wanted to do.

Yet, she could not shake this feeling of sadness. It was if she were leaving her best friend. Flashing herself an uneasy smile, she shook her head.

*That* certainly was not the case. She did not have any friends to speak of here—except for maybe the Tollivers. "Oh, Lizzy," she murmured regretfully. She clutched her brush to her breast. "I think I'll miss you the very most."

Her mind flitted back to the night the little girl had regained consciousness, when she and Joshua had last spoke. *And you, Joshua. However will I get through my days without seein' yer joyous and captivatin' brown eyes again?* "Why, oh, why couldn't things've worked out differn'tly for us?" she asked her reflection. "It woulda been so nice to—"

Her thoughts faltered. To what? Would she and Joshua have had any kind of a chance if she stayed? No. She took a deep breath, then moved to her satchel on the foot of the bed. She could not even make such a consideration. It was too painful.

Opening the bag, she carefully rolled the brush inside one of her buckskin garments, then tucked it safely inside. Well, no sense hanging back any longer. She might as well confront the inevitable and go downstairs to the breakfast table.

Spinning around, she headed for the door. A folded piece of paper lying beneath the gap on the floor caught her attention. She crossed the room and picked it up. Cautiously she opened the stationery and read:

## TO THE TOWNSHIP OF HARMONY

Today's Sunday services will be an open-air assembly held in the meadow on the west end

of town at the usual time of 10 A.M. Feel free
to bring a basket lunch, as we will be having a picnic social immediately following the
meeting.

> Looking forward to your joining us,
> Rev. Joshua Wylie

Puzzled, but pleased, DeeDee frowned. Could
this be the *surprise* he had spoken about the other
night? Was this the reason he had wanted her stay
in Harmony for a few more days? It had to be.
She refolded the paper and placed it inside her
dress pocket. Then, turning to the mirror, she gave
herself one last critical look.

She smoothed her hand down the lavender serge
gown she wore, then fluffed the dainty white lace
forming a *V* from her throat to her breastbone.
Shifting first one way, then the other, she checked
the matching sash, straightening it, though it did
not need it.

Ruth Alice and Rebecca could not find fault with
the way she was dressed today. In fact, since the
mishap with Lizzy, DeeDee had made certain that
they were hard-pressed to find any imperfection in
her attire, no flaw in her speech, no imperfection
in her actions. To all she came in contact with, she
appeared a lady in every respect. She had chosen to
show them that she *could* be a lady—but only when
*she* chose to be.

Satisfied with her appearance, she headed downstairs. The paper in her pocket crinkled as she
walked. She slowed her step. Pride swelled in
her heart. So Joshua was finally going to take

a chance. Smiling, she dipped her head. It was about time. Briefly she wondered how he would go about it.

She had seen him several times over the last few days, but he had respected her wishes and remained discreetly at a distance. Running her hand down the banister as she descended the steps, she sighed audibly. Too bad he was so considerate. She almost wished he had not been, now. She had missed talking to him these last few days.

She shrugged. It did not really matter, though. He probably would not have had any time for her, if she had not asked him to stay away from her. Every time she had seen him lately, it seemed he was always in too much of a hurry to pay her any attention.

And her father. He was up to some kind of mischief with Joshua—she knew it. The man was just as secretive, and always scurrying around with the minister. Why, if she had not seen the man from St. Joe's talking to Zeke about the barbershop, and had not, herself, witnessed the handshake that marked the sale of the shop, she might have suspected that her father was going back on his word and was plotting with Joshua to keep them in Harmony.

Female voices rose from the dining room.

DeeDee halted on the landing in the vestibule. Turning, she faced the closed door. *Only one more meal, DeeDee, girl.* She remembered the heroine's words when faced by hostiles in one of her favorite stories. *"Bravado and darin'. Hold the devils at bay. But, mind ya, act only on the defensive. . . ."*

Stiffening her spine, DeeDee marched forward. "Just one more meal," she murmured, bolstering her courage. "Sunday services for Joshua, and I'm on my way, then"—hand on the door, she paused— "San Francisco, here I come. . . ."

Standing at the edge of the same meadow where she and the children had caught Joshua practicing his sermon, she peered around at all of the murmuring people who had come from all over the farming community. Most of them she had not met, and now that she was leaving Harmony, she never would.

She clasped her hands at her back and leaned against a tree, pressing a palm hard upon the bark. She wanted to remember the feel of this place. Even with all the trouble she had been involved with here, she had to admit she was going to miss it. Even more so, she hated to acknowledge the fact that she was probably going to miss a lot of the people. She squinted against the brilliance of the sun.

Miss Maisie and Miss Minnie, ever adjoined with Rebecca and Ruth Alice, sat on a blanket spread near the front of the crowd.

From the corner of her eye, DeeDee saw the Tollivers—Nancy, Joey, and little Lizzy, too—waiting on a blanket at the opposite edge. She waved.

They returned her greeting.

At least Lizzy was doing better. The doctor had said she would not have the use of her arm for a short time while it healed, but the injury to her head did not appear to be serious anymore.

Glancing up at the position of the sun, she peered around at the other faces, wondering where her father could be. He had said he was coming. It had to be right at ten. Where was he? She had waited on the front porch of the boardinghouse as long as she could, but when everyone else had departed, and he still had not come for her, she took it upon herself to attend alone.

Like bees buzzing thick around a honeycomb, everyone either sat or stood, talking amongst themselves. Near as she could decipher, everyone had received the same kind of note as she had about Sunday service today. Sunday school for the children had even been canceled.

And where was Joshua? She could not see him anywhere. He had said this was a surprise, but if he did not show up soon—

Suddenly, off to one side, came a thunder of hoofbeats.

Startled, DeeDee cut a glance in the direction of the noise. She could not believe what she saw.

Racing toward the throng of expectant faces, Joshua rode astride a huge white stallion.

She blinked. At least, she thought it was Joshua.

The man who had just ridden in was dressed in boots, buckskin britches, and a matching fringed shirt with a beaded Indian belt at his waist.

She blinked again. Yeah, it was him all right.

In a fury of dust he skidded to a halt in front of the crowd. Leaping off the animal as if he were in a Wild West show, he whipped off a huge-brimmed cowboy hat, grinned, and bowed with dramatic flair. "Mornin', gents." He stooped in the other direction. "Ladies," he said, making pointed eye contact with Lillie Taylor.

"That ol' gal looks like she just found a rat'ler in her bedroll."

DeeDee whipped around to find her father grinning beside her. She darted a glance back at Joshua, then looked at Zeke. "What on earth's he up to?"

"Shh." Smirking, he nodded toward the minister. "The show's about to start."

DeeDee opened her mouth to question him further, but the sound of Joshua's voice snatched her attention to him.

Joshua let out a wild and blood-stirring war whoop, whipping his large white hat through the air. "Hear me children of the Lord. These six things does the Lord hate—yep—" He dipped his head and began pacing at the head of the congregation. "More'n anythin', too. Seven're a disgrace to him."

People cut each other shocked looks. They looked as though they thought he was crazy.

DeeDee, herself, was not completely certain he was not.

"So ye're askin' yerselves *what're* those abominations the Lord Almighty cain't abide? Well, friends, I'm here to tell ya. A proud look, a lyin' tongue, and hands that shed innocent blood. A heart that fabricates wicked stories, and feet that be swift in runnin' to mischief." He took a breath and hunched down a little. Then, squinting out of one eye, he looked directly at Billy Taylor, who sat with his mother and the rest of the Taylor clan, only a few feet from Minnie and Maisie. "He cain't stand a false witness who speaks lies about another'n, and he that causes discord amongst his feller men."

A rustle of murmurs rose up through the throng.

Still holding his hat, Joshua raised his hands. "I know, I know. Yer all wonderin' what in blazes has this got to do with you all? Well, sir—" He straightened to his full height and began to move throughout the crowd. "A long, long time ago there was this man, we'll call him Joe. Now Joe had himself a gang a men that ran all over this here countryside doin' nothin' but good fer ever'body they saw."

As DeeDee watched him, a slow smile grew across her entire face. He was doing it. He was actually preaching—here—today, just like he had when she had witnessed his practice. She peered around at the spectators.

Though most everybody wore an expression of wonder and disbelief, no one spoke. Not even a whisper rose up around her.

"Now, after years an' years a bein' a friend, a teacher, a doctor, an' a preacher to ever'body he ever knew, do you all know what happened to this here Joe?" he asked.

Most everyone shook their heads.

Joshua dashed over to where Joey Tolliver knelt watching, and squatted down. "What about you, podner? Do *you* know?"

With huge eyes staring at Joshua, Joey only replied with a small wag of his head.

"Well, sir, his own men practically handed him straight over to some really bad *hombres* called— um—Romans, I think they was. Yep." He nodded, then jumped up again. "Ya see, these here Romans wanted ol' Joe real bad. They didn't take to no contradictin' what they declared was law, and well, them laws they made was awful. And ol' Joe, he knew they was bad."

"How'd he know, Reverend Wylie?" Joey asked, his little voice quivering with anticipation.

"Well, boy, 'cause his daddy done told him the truth of the way things was s'pose to be a long time afore that."

"Just 'cause his daddy told him it was so, don't make it right—"

"Joey!" Nancy Tolliver yanked on the child's sleeve.

The boy flinched, then looked back at Joshua. Apparently thoroughly chastised, he swallowed. "Does it?" he asked in a meeker tone.

Joshua laughed aloud.

The congregation chuckled with him.

"Don't you know when things're right an' when they ain't?"

Joey nodded.

"What about you? And you?" he asked others.

They all answered the same as Joey.

"An' didn't yer mamas an' daddies teach all of you the wrong an' right of things?"

All heads bobbed as one.

Zeke moved up closer. "He's good, ain't he?" he whispered in DeeDee's ear.

Keeping to silence, she only smiled. She did not want to miss even one word Joshua spoke.

"Ya know, ol' Joe, he died that day, at the hands of them Romans. An' all a'cause of his *proud*, so-called friends, that *lied*, and whose *hearts fabricated wicked stories*, and whose *feet couldn't wait to run an' tell on him.* And Joe—" Joshua spun around and shook his fist, glaring at his parishioners as he did so. "He was kilt by the *hands that shed His innocent blood*—them Romans' hands."

DeeDee sucked in a breath. Where was he going with all of this? Where was the lesson he hoped to teach?

"Now my question to you, ladies and gents, is what kind of friend're you?" He moved deeper into the throng. "Would you let yerself swell up with pride so bad ya'd lie against a friend of yers?" he asked Hutton Kincaid.

"Nah, sir. I wouldn't."

"And you." Joshua wheeled on Alexander Evans. "Do you have a heart that would fabricate wicked stories against yer neighbor?"

"Not mine," the man answered.

"Uh-huh." Pushing on through the onlookers, Joshua moved to Ruth Alice. "And you, sister." He bent down on one knee. "Do ya have feet that cain't wait to run and tell on another of yer brethren?"

She didn't reply, keeping her eyes downcast.

"And you, Lillie Taylor." He shifted toward the woman. "How do *you* feel about those that would shed an innocent's blood?"

DeeDee could only see Mrs. Taylor's profile, but even from that she could tell that the woman was completely at a loss for words.

"Well, now," Joshua hollered as he lurched back up. "What would ya say if I told ya that ever' single one of ya was just like Joe's friends?"

"How so, Reverend?" a man yelled, his tone angry.

"How so, brother?" Joshua pointed at him. "There are those in this town who're seeking to spill this innocent's blood with their self-righteous talk and accusing words."

DeeDee nearly choked on a breath. He was talking about her.

"No," another called out.

"Yes." Joshua swept an implicating finger over the heads of the congregation. "Maybe not true blood, but it might as well be. You're all running her out of town, and why? Because she's different." He started to walk toward her with slow, deliberate steps.

All heads turned her way.

DeeDee moved back a space.

Zeke barred her escape.

"No, Papa, please," she whispered fearfully. "Don't let this happen. Get me out of here please."

"Just wait, girl. The boy knows what he's doin'."

DeeDee cringed. So it was true. Her own father was in on this ridiculous plan of Joshua's.

"She's just like our friend, Joe. But by now you've probably all figured out that the man in my story was actually our Lord and Savior, Jesus Christ."

"Are you tellin' us that that young woman, that Delilah Gallagher, is like Jesus Christ Himself?" a woman cried out.

DeeDee could not see her, but she suspected it was Lillie Taylor. She clutched her hands together to thwart their shaking, but it did no good. She was trembling all over. Why was he singling her out like this? This would only make matters worse.

"She's as gentle and pure of heart, and filled with nothing but pure love for her fellow man." He halted midstride and shot a glance over his shoulder. "Even for those who would hold only contempt for her."

"Amen, Reverend Wylie." It was Nancy Tolliver's voice that rose up this time. Nodding with obvious approval, she smiled at DeeDee.

"True, she rode into Harmony in a flurry of buckskin. You thought she looked different, and talked different." He turned back and resumed his course toward her. "Some of you only saw what was on the outside. And when you heard her name—well, that was all that was necessary to condemn her there and then. But what you missed—what you never took time to get to know—" He smiled as he drew nearer, his eyes twinkling with that same alluring charm they always had whenever he looked at her.

DeeDee felt her face heat. Her heart was pounding so hard she thought it would surely leap out of her breast.

"Was that under those odd clothes she always

wore is a warm and giving heart. And beyond that frontier language she tossed around is a lady of rare quality." He stopped again and peered out over the crowd. "Now, it's my understanding that there's been a certain little matchmaking game going on around town."

The spectators gasped as one.

Maisie and Minnie exchanged a guilty look.

"Oh, yes, I know about it. And actually—" He paused. "I'm really quite glad about it. It made me realize that I truly *do* need a wife."

As before with the gasp, an audible sigh of relief rustled through the flock.

"And—" he said with emphasis, his gaze narrowing back on her.

DeeDee held her breath. *No, Joshua,* she pleaded silently, *don't do it.* She tried to move off to the side, but Zeke stopped her again.

"Hold still, girl. Hear the man out," he mumbled loud enough so that only she could hear him.

Great, so Joshua was a *man* now. A moment ago he was just a boy.

"I've made my choice of a bride."

*Oh, God, please. Ya can't let this happen to me— not now—not like this.* She was so embarrassed, yet so overjoyed at the prospect that he might actually ask her to marry him, she did not know whether to be angry or elated.

Moving up directly in front of her, Joshua bent on one knee. He tossed his hat to the ground, then grabbed hold of her hand.

She tried to pull away, but he held on fast. "Papa, please." She glanced at Zeke over her shoulder. "Help me."

He shook his head and grinned, then winked at Joshua. "I done my part in all a this. You two're on yer own now."

"Papa!" DeeDee shouted. But it was of no use.

Zeke had moved off to stand with the Tolliver family.

"Delilah Gallagher?"

Startled, DeeDee stared back at Joshua.

"It would be my greatest hon'r—" He switched to his earlier Wild West dialect. "If'n ya'd consider to be my wife."

Trembling worse than she had been before, DeeDee closed her eyes. *This can't be happening*, she repeated in her mind.

Silence reigned.

"DeeDee?" Joshua's voice came to her again. Apparently, he had meant what he had asked. He was not letting this go.

Now what was she going to do?

"DeeDee, look at me," he demanded softly. He clutched her hand tighter. "I love you, DeeDee. And I can't think of any better gift you could give me than to love me enough back to say yes."

Hesitantly she opened her eyes. Had he spoken the truth? "We—we've only known each other a week, Joshua," she said in a whimper. "How can you be in love with me?"

He shrugged, his lips twitching mischievously

at the corners. "I don't know, but I just am." He
squeezed her hand. He peered up at her with sincere eyes.

Oh, God. It was true. She could see it in the way
he looked at her. Her heart soared. She had known
even before the other night in the kitchen of the
boardinghouse that she was in love with him—
desperately, hopelessly in love with him—but she
was afraid to tell him. Afraid that if she did he
might do something—something just like this.

"So will you, DeeDee?" He swallowed hard, causing his Adam's apple to bob.

From out of the corner of her eye, she saw her
father lean down and carefully lift Lizzy into his
arms.

The little girl waved again and grinned gleefully.
"S-s-say ye-yes, DeeDee."

The crowd chuckled as one.

Joshua nodded. "Say yes, DeeDee."

Confronted by her own feelings, DeeDee felt a
flood of confusion. She knew she loved him, but
she did not want to ruin his reputation with the
congregation, and with the way everybody felt
about her—

"Say yes, DeeDee," Nancy Tolliver called out.

"Say yes, DeeDee!" Maisie and Minnie yelled.

A moment later another echoed their words.

Followed by another, and still another. Then, one
by one, each person within the crowd stood and
voiced the same plea. "Say yes, DeeDee. Say yes."

Tears filled her eyes as she peered at the faces

before her. Her throat closed.

Even Lillie and Billy Taylor were chanting the request.

How had this happened to her? And why? She looked down at Joshua. What should she do? Zeke. She glanced at him.

Grinning with a smile that bespoke utter satisfaction, he answered her unasked question with a nod.

The voices grew louder, until DeeDee thought she would burst with the pure thunder of their voices.

Joshua rose to his full height, then pulled her into his embrace. "Say yes, DeeDee."

She held to silence one last second, then—"Yes!" she shouted as loud as she could. "Yes," she repeated, quieter, private, and only for him. But her whisper was lost amidst the rumble of applause.

Joshua must have heard her, for his face nearly glowed with happiness. He kissed her softly. "I love you, Delilah Gallagher."

"I thought we decided it was DeeDee—no Miss— no Delilah, just DeeDee." She grinned impishly. "And I love you, too." Still in awe of how this had all come about, she shook her head and hugged him to her.

Here in this little meadow, outside of the small town of Harmony, divine intervention had surely prevailed on this circle of people.

Leaning back a space, she peered into Joshua's handsome face. Filled with more joy than words could ever convey, DeeDee clutched Joshua tighter and squeezed. Never would she have believed this could happen—not here—not with these people as witnesses, and certainly not to her. Through tear-filled eyes, she glanced at all the smiling faces of Harmony, Kansas.

# UNDER THE SHELL

### The Amazing Grace of Delilah Gallagher

By Billy Taylor

KANSAS—A little over one week after the arrival of Miss Delilah (DeeDee) Gallagher finds Harmony's long-standing Ladies' Auxiliary planning a wedding. And although in the tradition of her namesake Miss Gallagher has taken every opportunity to *crop the hair* of the resident womenfolk, and sent them into a dither of constant what-to-dos, the town is pleased to announce the marriage between Reverend Joshua Wylie and the same Miss Delilah Gallagher.

For although she sometimes faltered under the same pretext as her predecessor, what with baptizing the previously named minister more than once, and constantly upsetting the townsfolk with her many *amazing* storytelling talents, it has been proved, and rather painfully, too, that she is a true asset to the community through her love and generosity.

And though this reporter, himself, has butted heads more than once with Miss Gallagher, it is his opinion that Delilah Gallagher should be renamed Amazing Grace. Thank you, DeeDee, for all that you've taught us in Harmony. We wish you all the best.


UPDATE

For those of you who did not attend last Sunday's services, Miss Gallagher and Reverend Wylie announced their wedding would take place just as soon as their house was finished being built.

EXTRA

Zeke Gallagher would like to announce that he has taken on a new partner from St. Joe's. So all of you that have a hankering for a haircut, or a rankling toothache, be sure to stop by the bright yellow building on Main Street, located next to Miss Minnie and Miss Maisie's boardinghouse.

# FREE
# Romance
## *(a $4.50 value)*

### Send in the Coupon Below

To get your FREE historical romance and start saving, fill out the coupon below and mail it today. As soon as we receive it we'll send you your FREE Book along with your first month's selections.